Our Moment

Our Moment

Michael Clark

New York | Los Angeles | London | Sydney

ISBN: 979-8-88581-224-5 Hardback
ISBN: 979-8-88581-225-2 Paperback
ISBN: 979-8-88581-226-9 eBook

Michael Clark

Dedication

To Josette, for bringing purpose and balance to my life,
the glue that held the pieces together
when it mattered most.

To Keyan, Kaylyn, and Buddy, for adding joy
and a touch of chaos to every chapter of this journey.

And to my parents, for their endless belief
and unwavering support,
my greatest PR agents.

Michael Clark

Michael Clark

Table of Contents

Prologue
The Flicker Before the Flame

The world didn't stop.
It just changed so quietly that no one noticed.

It felt like the moment before a spark, the flicker before
something caught fire.
Not flames, but futures.
A glitch we chose not to see.

Life carried on. But the pattern shifted.
The codes beneath our lives began to rewrite themselves
changing what we saw, what we bought, even what we
remembered.

But some of us felt it
like a thread had come loose, and the fabric of our lives was
slowly unravelling.

One of them was a boy named Esra.
He didn't have power. Or a platform.
But he began to notice the gaps, in what we were being told, in
what we were losing.
And when no one else asked the question, he did.
The story you're about to read is his.
But it might also be yours.

I didn't write this book because I had all the answers.
Before all of this, I wrote a paper that opened my eyes.
I saw a path others didn't.

Since then, I've watched a playlist disappear.
A job be replaced.
A voice go silent.
People left behind.
And the chasm continues to grow.

And yet, many called it progress.

Michael Clark

This book begins with a question
one that wouldn't leave me alone:

What if we're missing something?
What if intelligence, real, human intelligence, isn't something to automate away, but to elevate?

What if data isn't just a resource to mine, but a reflection of who we are?
And what if the machines we've built aren't the threat . . . but the mirror?

What you're about to read is not just a story.
It's a reminder of what we once had, and what we still might become.
A glimpse of what could be,
if we dare to act.

And when you turn the final page,
I'll be there, waiting,
so we can finally understand
why this is **Our Moment**.

Michael Clark

Michael Clark

PART I
Visioning –
An Idea and a Belief

Dream That Stayed

"Somewhere, something incredible
is waiting to be known."
— Carl Sagan

The rain wasn't real.
Not entirely.

It fell in a steady rhythm, artificially seeded to cleanse the air, wash the streets, and keep the illusion of order alive.

Tracing the edges of glass towers, sliding like veins down mirrored skin, bending neon into liquid streaks.
Holographic billboards shimmered as droplets passed through them, distorting flawless smiles that blinked without meaning.

Beneath his feet, millions of invisible transactions pulsed through underground servers, predicting, adjusting, learning with every breath its citizens took.

The boy felt it, in the tightness behind his ribs, the way silence followed him in crowded rooms.

He didn't know what it meant, only that everything moved too perfectly.
The trains arrived the moment he stepped onto the platform.
Stores showed him products he'd only thought about.

News shifted, headlines rewriting mid-sentence, depending on who was watching.
It was seamless. Convenient. Effortless.
And yet, it unsettled him.

Not in a way he could explain, just a quiet itch at the base of his skull, like something watching.

Esra had always seen patterns no one else noticed, threads between the silence and the noise.

While his friends hurled themselves headfirst into tech, Esra hung back, not afraid, just quietly aware.

At school, he'd sit at the edge of the bench, fingers curled over the fraying straps of his bag, watching them scroll.
His nails were bitten. A thread on his sleeve tugged loose and forgotten.
He looked young. Most days, he felt older than all of them.

Like the only one still awake while the dream played on.
They filtered their faces, posted clips from old films they swore they'd seen.
Esra hadn't. Sometimes, he wasn't even sure they had.

Their feeds pulsed with headlines tailored just for them; updates he couldn't trace.
None of it was strange. Not to them.
Sometimes, it felt like he was standing just outside something, watching the world bend around him.

Everything felt . . . tailored.
Words changed depending on who was near.
The past blurred at the edges, like a file rewritten in silence.

The thought hovered. Then vanished. Like a window closed in his mind.

It started small.
One morning, his favourite playlist vanished.
Photos he'd taken, gone.
The next day, his news feed reset. Like he'd never existed.
His apps no longer recognised him. Even his messages felt . . . hollow, like replies from someone else's life.

At first, it looked like a glitch.
A reset. A bug in the feed.
But then, he tried to log in.
And the system didn't just lock him out;
It acted like he was never there at all.

Michael Clark

That morning, the turnstile at the station didn't open.
The scanner flashed red.
Not declined.
Unrecognised.

A guard looked past him. Commuters flowed around like he
wasn't there.
It was small. But it rattled something deep.

A company he'd signed up for years ago vanished overnight.
Its data absorbed. Its records erased.
And with it, a version of Esra disappeared.
No warning. No message. Just gone.

His preferences. His history.
All those small pieces of himself he'd fed into machines
swept away without a trace.

And yet, nothing really changed.
His friends didn't notice.
His teachers didn't care.
Even the systems that once tracked his every move simply
moved on, as if he'd never been there at all.

He was still here.
But it felt like . . . less of him was.

For the first time, the boy felt a different kind of emptiness.
Not like losing a thing.
More like losing a reflection.

He didn't have the words for it yet.
Just a feeling.
A quiet sense that something had slipped away
and no one even looked back.

Then, just for a moment
he saw them.
Children playing in the rain.
But it wasn't their laughter that stopped him.

It was the colour.
One of them wore a yellow coat.

The kind of yellow you only see in sunlight or memory.
It wasn't just bright.
It was defiant, in a world that had forgotten how to shine.

She turned, just for a second.
Met his eyes.
Smiled.

And then she was gone
like a glitch in the system.

The street was empty again.
The rain kept falling.
But the world didn't feel the same.

That moment stayed with him all day. But it was that night the world began to unravel.
Esra sat at the kitchen table,
listening to the low hum of the city pressing against the windows.
Then, her phone rang.

His mother answered.
Her voice was calm.
Too calm.

"I understand the decision."
A pause. A nod, slow and hollow.
Then, a shift, barely noticeable.
"But . . . a machine is replacing me?"

Silence.

"What about everything I know?"
"All I've done?"

Another silence.

"Of course."

She set the phone down gently.
Sat still.
And then she smiled.

Not because she was okay.
But because she'd already accepted it.

A week later, she worked longer hours.
A month later, she changed medications.
A year later
She was someone else.

Esra never said it aloud, but that night rewrote something in him.
He couldn't stop it.
But maybe next time . . .
Maybe next time he could.

That night he slept. He dreamt.
Of a very different world.
A world where his mother still had her job.
Where the machine beside her helped, but didn't replace.
Where she still mattered.
Where she was still his mother.

A world where his data wasn't gone.
Where the music he had saved, the messages he had sent, still belonged to him.
Where he wasn't erased.
A world where people knew what was real.

Where no one's choices could be rewritten, erased, or lost.
It was just a dream.
But when he woke, it stayed with him.
A quiet thought, taking root.

The dream hadn't left him.
The systems outside now acted like the people in it.
They didn't know who he was.

He sat up in bed, chest heaving.
The room was still, but his thoughts weren't.

How can something be gone if I never even understood what it was?
The dream was fading, but the feeling clung to him, like mist on his skin.

Like something inside had cracked, and the silence rushing in was louder than anything he'd ever heard.

Maybe it was just a dream.
But his playlists were gone. His feeds were blank.
The system had forgotten him.

What if forgetting me . . . was the point?
That night, as the hum deepened and the shadows stretched long across the walls, the world began to blur again.
Reality softened. And something else slipped in.

How does that even happen?
He rubbed his face, hands trembling without permission.
He wanted to laugh. Or scream. Or wake up again.

But the world outside hadn't changed.
Which meant either he was breaking . . .
Or everything else was.

What if the world didn't have to be this way?
What if we could be . . . more?

And then, the next night, the dream returned.
Not exactly the same.
Clearer. Stronger.

And as the days passed, the world around him felt colder and emptier.
Like he was watching it through glass.
Like something was calling him from the other side.
Then, one night, the dream changed.

The world wasn't golden anymore.
It wasn't full of light, of possibility.
It was crumbling.

The streets cracked.
The buildings flickered, their edges breaking apart like ash in the wind.
Esra jolted awake.
His heart was racing.
His hands clenched the sheets.

Michael Clark

The dream wasn't just a dream anymore.
It was a message.
And it wasn't going to stop.

Something was slipping away.
Something was being lost before he even knew what it was.
Outside, the city moved as it always had.

The same rain. The same lights.
The same hum of invisible systems running the world.
But Esra wasn't sure if it was the world that had changed . . .
or if he had.

He wasn't dreaming anymore.
The world was.
And if he didn't wake up, no one would.
He had to find the answers.
Before it was too late.

He didn't know where to begin.
But he knew he couldn't stay still.

For a moment, he thought about letting it go.
Letting the world forget him.
Maybe that would be easier.

To slip beneath the noise and be nothing at all.
But then he saw her face again.
Not the girl in the coat
His mother.

The smile that wasn't real.
The silence that followed.
And something inside him refused.

Michael Clark

Book That Was Waiting

"Not all those who wander are lost."

— J.R.R. Tolkien

The next morning, the silence lingered.
Not the peaceful kind
but the kind that follows something you can't explain.

The dream still clung to him,
the glitch, the girl, the weight behind his mother's smile.
He didn't know what it meant.

The morning felt different.
Not because anything had changed,
but because everything felt too much the same.
Rain still fell in perfect rhythm.

The streets moved in their endless loops.
The city hummed, watching, listening.
Still, something in him had shifted.
Something was waiting.

He walked without knowing where he was going
Through streets he had walked a thousand times.
Past stores that knew what he wanted.

His coat hung loose, sleeves too long, like it once belonged to
someone else. Straight black hair slipped across his brow, always
a little untidy no matter how he tried to fix it.

A boy, still. But only just.
Caught between disappearing . . . and becoming.

Today, he ignored the stores.
Followed a feeling. A pull.

At the corner of the plaza, a store's security gate chimed
as he passed even though he hadn't gone inside.

The scanner chirped. Red.
He hadn't touched anything.
A few heads turned. A man stepped back like he'd caught
something.
Esra didn't speak.
He didn't have to.

It wasn't his voice they reacted to.
it was something else.
Like for a second,
they saw the rhythm break.
Not because of him.
Because of themselves.

And then, he saw it.
A bookshop.

Small. Wedged between two towering buildings, its sign
flickering like a dying thought.

He had passed this street so many times.
And yet, never seen this place before.

The window was lined with books from no particular time.
No digital displays. Just worn pages and leather-bound spines.
Something about it felt out of place.

Or maybe, he thought, it was the only thing that belonged.
He pushed the door open.
The bell above the entrance didn't ring.

The shop didn't feel like it was meant to be found, more like it
had been waiting for the right person to open it.

Inside, the air smelled of dust and old paper, the kind of scent
that didn't exist in the city anymore.
The shelves stretched high, packed with untouched books.
Some titles were faded. Some had no titles at all.

Michael Clark

And behind the counter, a man watched him.
Not in the way storekeepers did.
He wasn't waiting to sell something.
He was waiting for someone.

His jacket looked like it had belonged to another century, heavy brown wool and the collar slightly frayed. A pair of cracked glasses dangled from a leather cord around his neck, though he didn't seem to need them.

One of his shoes was scuffed, the other almost new.
Like he'd walked two different roads to get here.

His face was marked with age, not in lines, but in stillness, like time had tried to press itself into him.

Something told him that once he stepped further inside, once he crossed this threshold there would be no going back.
His fingers curled. Slowly, he stepped forward.

The bookseller's gaze didn't waver.
He didn't greet the boy. Didn't ask if he needed help.
Instead, he simply studied him, as if trying to place him in time.

Esra swallowed. The silence pressed in. He suddenly felt small beneath the weight of those eyes.

"You look like someone carrying a question," the man said finally.

His voice had the softness of paper, dry, slow, deliberate. The kind of voice that filled a room without ever needing to rise.

Esra blinked. "What?"

The bookseller didn't move. "People come here for different reasons."

He shifted slightly, resting both hands on the counter like someone who'd stood there too long. "Some want stories. Some want answers. And some . . . " He narrowed his eyes, " . . . don't know what they want. Only that something's missing."

A draft passed through the store, rustling the pages of a book on a nearby shelf. Esra glanced at it, unsettled.

"I was just looking," he said, more quickly than he meant to.
The man reached behind him and flipped the wooden sign on the door, "Closed."
"Were you?"

Esra turned away, pretending to scan the titles.

The air smelled dry, leather, dust, and something metallic.
But he wasn't really reading.

Because he could feel those eyes still on him.
"Why do you hesitate?"
"I don't."
"You do."
Esra's jaw tightened. The light overhead flickered.

"You think too much before you act," the bookseller said, stepping out from behind the counter. His footsteps barely made a sound.
"Afraid of believing in something too much because, what if you're wrong?"

"That's not true."
"Isn't it?"

The man was now standing just a few feet away, hands behind his back.
"The world around you, it moves too perfectly. Gives you everything you need before you ask.

But something inside you keeps whispering . . . "
He leaned slightly closer, voice quieter.

" . . . what if this isn't the way it was meant to be?"
Esra's skin prickled.
Those words, he had thought them. Not out loud. Never out loud.

"I don't know what you're talking about," he said. But the words felt hollow, like they belonged to someone else.

The bookseller smiled, not unkindly, but like someone seeing through fog. "I think you do."

Michael Clark

A siren passed, muted, like the city was folding in on itself.
Esra looked away. His fingers trailed across a cracked spine.

"The world teaches you to doubt," the man went on.
"To believe some things are impossible simply because they
haven't been done yet."

"That's not . . . " Esra stopped.
Because he had heard that before.
Not from someone else.
From himself.

In the dreams. In the static. In the quiet between thoughts.
"It's just a dream," he muttered.
The bookseller tilted his head. "What if it isn't?"

Esra said nothing.
"They're just dreams."
"Yet you keep having the same one."

A floorboard creaked. The bookseller turned and walked toward
a shelf near the back of the store.

Esra hadn't noticed before.
Unlike the others, it was almost empty.
"Someone left this," the bookseller said, fingers brushing over the
frame. "A long time ago."

He paused, as if listening to something the walls remembered.
"It's not my job to understand it," he said softly, more to the
room than to Esra. "Only to keep the door from closing."

Then, as if finishing a sentence:
"They said someone like you might come in one day."

Esra stepped closer. The book in the man's hands didn't shine or
glow. It simply was.

Worn leather. No title. No markings.
The bookseller placed it gently on the counter.

"You're later than I expected," the bookseller said softly to
himself, as if commenting on a clock no one else could see.

Esra blinked.
He gave a small, breathless laugh.
Not joy, more like disbelief.
"You make it sound like I'm late for a dentist appointment."

The bookseller didn't smile, but something in his gaze softened.
"Time arrives when it's ready. Not before."

The bookseller slid the book toward him.
"Take it."

Esra hesitated.
"What if I don't?"

The man smirked, like he'd heard this question before many times.
"Then nothing changes. The city hums. The rain falls.
And you keep wondering why the dream won't let you go."

Esra's fingers closed around the book. It felt heavier than it should.
"If I open it . . . what happens?"

The man's expression didn't change.
"You already know the answer."
Silence. Not empty, charged.
"This book . . . what is it?"

The bookseller exhaled slowly.

"I've never been able to open it."
Then, looking at Esra, not as a boy, but as something more. "But
you will know what to do."

"And if I don't?

"Then you were never meant to."
Esra stared at him.
"That's it?" he asked. "Not save the world, not you're
the chosen one?"
He glanced at the book, brow raised slightly.

"Just . . . read?"

The bookseller gave the smallest smile.

Michael Clark

"Every story begins the same way."

The book felt heavier than it should. Like it wasn't just paper and ink, but something waiting to be understood.

He turned toward the door.
The store felt smaller now.
Like the books were listening.

He didn't look back.
"She gave you more than a smile, you know," the bookseller said softly.
A pause, thick as memory.

"She gave you the reason you still don't understand . . .
. . . but you will."

Esra froze.
Not because of the words.
But because part of him already knew they were true.

He let out a breath he hadn't realised he'd been holding.
It rested in his arms like it belonged there, and always had.

PART 2

Discovering
The Untold Story

A Journey Begins

"To know the past is to guide the future."

— Confucius

The bell above the door didn't ring.
The moment he stepped out, the city swallowed him whole.

The streets stretched longer. Billboards glared too perfect. The city's hum felt too precise.
He stepped into a dream he no longer belonged to.

The air smelled sharp, like metal and memory.
The kind of scent that lingered in cities that had forgotten they were once forests.

He inhaled slowly. Something about it felt . . . hollow.
Manufactured. Even the weather seemed scripted.

The boy clutched the book tighter. He glanced back. The bookseller stood in the window, watching.

Then . . . the lights inside flickered once . . . then vanished. The store melted into the night, absorbed by the city's glow. And for the first time, he felt truly alone.

The city blurred behind him, a river of neon and noise.
Esra slipped into a narrow alley without thinking.
It was barely wide enough for one person.

Cracked walls climbed around him, slick with rain.
Above, a streetlamp hummed, casting tired yellow light on the broken pavement.

The boy slid down against the wall and pulled the book close.
It felt heavier now, like it knew.

His fingers hovered, cold, damp, unsteady. Then he opened it. The first page caught the light. Simple. Unmistakable.

A handwritten line slashed across the margin: "This isn't history. It's a memory we forgot we left behind."

He blinked. His breath caught. The message felt personal. Not meant for everyone. Meant for someone who had been asleep. Someone like him.

"Our Untold History." No author. Just worn pages. Drawings and notes scattered like lost voices.

He squinted. "No title page. No barcode. Okay . . . mysterious forbidden text it is."

He turned the page. "The Beginning." Not a spark. Not a single moment. Something older. Something deeper. Something that connected them all.

No tech. No machines.

Only cave paintings. The kind he'd skimmed past in school, chalky shapes on a holo-board, explained away in seconds.

But here . . . The rough sketches breathed. Their colours, dulled by time, still pulsed with life in a way the world no longer did.

A tremor of recognition. Not memory, something stranger. Like remembering a dream he never had.

"Memories. Stories. Relationships."

The words beneath the image blurred.
He blinked.
The air thickened, or maybe his chest tightened.

A musty scent curled up from the paper,
dust, leather, and something earthy, like ash after rain.
Maps sketched in sand.
Moments etched in stone.

Symbols passed hand-to-hand, long before machines spoke for us.

Michael Clark

Then, scrawled across the margin in uneven letters: "Data wasn't born with machines. It was born with us."
The line stopped him.
Everything, the damp alley walls, the yellow lamplight, the city's hum, dropped away.

"What does that even mean?" he muttered. "And why does it feel like it's talking to me?" He shook his head. "This is insane. Data? Since when is data sacred?"

Esra flipped pages back and forth. A scowl curled his mouth. "This isn't about me," he said, anchoring himself. But something inside whispered, Then why can't you stop reading?

He kept turning the pages. Each one felt like crossing a line he couldn't return from. History surged like a river cracking through stone. With every footprint, every fire lit, every whispered story under stars, humanity left a trail.

And now, somehow,
Esra held it.
Not just existence.
Dreams. Becoming.

Forget social media, the words said.
Our first posts were scratched into dust and blood.

A page faded at the edges, as if time tried to erase it.
Europe's caves: France. Spain. 40,000 years ago.
He skimmed this in school. But never felt it. Now, the words dragged him underground.

He almost saw it, endless darkness

Air thick with stone and ash.

Walls flickering by firelight in trembling hands. Horses. Antelope.
Handprints in ochre and ash, not decorations. Proof. I was here.

"Lascaux." Discovered in 1940.

But waiting so much longer.
A chill cut through him.
Not pictures, portals carved through time.

Windows into fear. Into prayer.
Into the ache of remembering.
Long before we spoke in words, we spoke in data.

"Data wasn't a thing," one line whispered. "It was a gift."
He blinked. He had never thought of it like that.

Data, to him, meant numbers. Noise.
Machine-stuff.
But now, it felt human.
Handprints. Charcoal. Lines carved in stone.
It was all a kind of memory.
A signal.

He looked up. The city kept pulsing, glass, metal, digital ghosts.
But this page showed him something deeper.

The leather felt warm, like it had held the firelight.
Rain slid down his face.
He barely noticed.

Time didn't pass. It folded.
He turned the page.

The sands whispered next, Egypt.
Pyramids, scrolls, stories etched in eternity.

Where once they painted with pigment, now they carved with
symbols. Hieroglyphics etched in stone. Sacred. Precise. Scrolls
pressed between fingers. Stories stretched across eternity.

Suddenly, a loud clatter, metal and plastic, made him flinch.
A bag of trash slammed against a nearby wall, tossed from a
window above.
Someone shouted, then a door slammed.

A reflex said: Close the book.
Run. This is too weird. "This isn't history," he muttered. "Just
weird. Just . . . cryptic."

Michael Clark

He froze. Was someone watching? A shadow flickered, but when he looked up, nothing.
His hands stayed. The book hummed in them like it connected to something inside him.

He closed his eyes. Rain streaked across his cheeks. And for a moment, he heard it. The scrape of a chisel. The whisper of a brush.
The past speaking. Not for profit. Not for power. Because they knew. Data mattered. Because it was identity.

He opened his eyes. The world around him deepened. Not with fear, but gravity. Older. More alive.

The Rosetta Stone. 196 BCE

He remembered someone calling it the first Translate tool, a stone that unlocked civilizations.

A decree carved in three scripts. Three languages.
One message. Data wasn't hoarded. It was shared, so anyone, anywhere, could understand. A bridge to the future. A message to unborn hands. A gift.

He almost laughed, not from joy, but from the ache of recognition.
Data wasn't a commodity. It wasn't a weapon. It was life. It was trust. It was a birthright.

He pressed his hand against the old stone wall beside him. It thrummed with rain. With memory.

The past wasn't far. It stood beside him. Still whispering.
The book wasn't done. Ancient Greece. Markets bustled. Open debates. Ink and scroll.
Data evolved again. Not just preserving what was, but shaping what could be.

Socrates. Plato. Aristotle.

They didn't just preserve knowledge. They sharpened it. Challenged it. Forged it into philosophy, science, law.

Even before the printing presses. Before copyright. They understood.

Data wasn't just fact. It was force. It was how civilization breathed.
A word blinked from the page, "Datum." Latin. Gift.

Rain streaked through his hair. His collar, soaked. His fingers trembled, not from cold, but from the word's weight. He whispered, "Gift . . . "

A chill rippled through him. "Of course it meant gift," he said. "It always had."
Not just a file. Not a number. A memory. A bridge. A gift passed from hand to hand, to people not yet born.

And suddenly, he understood. And it cracked something open.

His stomach knotted. Doubt crept in. What had once been shared . . . now felt hoarded. Twisted. Sold.

He swallowed hard. A flicker of betrayal sparked through the awe. Had we forgotten? Had we stopped seeing data as life, and started using it as leverage?
A breeze swept the alley. A paper cup scraped across wet stone. The city groaned in the distance, sirens, static and the clatter of footsteps.

Another word caught the light, "Identitas." State of being.
A drawing spelled it out: Data wasn't separate from us. It was us. Two sides of the same coin: Identity and data.

Memory and meaning. Existence and worth. All connected.
Esra exhaled. He rose. The book pressed tight to his chest. His clothes soaked. The chill finally reached him.
The alley stretched, narrow, endless, waiting. Above, the streetlamp flickered . . . then steadied.

He stepped into the open.
The book still weighed on him. Not to crush, to remind.
The question clung to him. Why him? He was just a boy. Almost a man. But still a boy.

Not a scholar. Not a leader. Why had the book found him?

He didn't know. But he stepped forward anyway. One step. Then another.
He felt it in his bones. This was bigger than him. Bigger than the book. Bigger than dreams whispered to rain

He didn't ask for this. But it had found him anyway.
He didn't know what it was yet, only that something had begun.

And he would need help. Not just anyone.
Someone who could see the invisible cracks. Someone who still believed in a boy with a dream.

Michael Clark

4
Measure of Time

"The more precisely you measure time,
the more you realize it cannot be measured"
— *Carlo Rovelli*

The rain hadn't stopped, just thinned into a whisper.

Esra walked. Still night. Still not home. The air curled around him, thick with memory.

A question pressed at his ribs like a stone in his pocket.

Who is that someone?
The one who might believe in this . . . in him?

Was it foolish to think he mattered in all this? Or was this the start of something older?

He moved without thinking, into motion, into light, rain-slick rubber beneath his feet.

A horn. Headlights.
"Watch it, kid!"

Stumbling across the road. Heart pounding. Breath sharp. He hadn't even looked. Hadn't even cared.

He hadn't thought if anyone even knew he was gone. This was bigger now. Bigger than phone calls. Bigger than home.

But bigger than one boy? That, he wasn't ready to admit.

Then, like a signal tuning in, a name surfaced, Theo.

He didn't know who Theo was. Not really. Not a teacher. Not family.
But once, years ago, Theo had looked at him like he wasn't broken. Like he was worth finding.

Theo didn't raise him. Didn't rescue him. Didn't owe him anything.
And that's what made Esra trust him.

He remembered the smell of Theo's study, dust, old paper, candle wax.
A room untouched by time. Or maybe protected by it.

Notebooks crammed onto shelves; maps pinned in no discernible order, like Theo could see a world no one else dared imagine.

Theo hadn't just preserved history. He argued with it.
Lived inside it. Challenged it to do better.

"If anyone could help him make sense of this feeling, this strange, heavy object . . . it was Theo."

Esra dug into his pocket, pulled out his battered phone. His thumb hovered. The screen flickered under the rain.

The number was still there, buried under a year of silence.
He tapped it.

One ring.
Then a voice broke through, warm, familiar, like firelight after a storm.

"Esra," Theo said. "No need to explain."
A beat.
"I was expecting you."

Esra froze. The city fell away, just the soft static of rain between them.

Was this fate? Or had something already decided this path long ago?
". . . Where are you?" he asked.

Theo's voice was soft, almost smiling, like he'd been waiting years for this exact moment. "The old station. Platform Nine. The trains stopped coming years ago . . . but I never left."

The line went dead.

Michael Clark

Esra stood for a heartbeat longer, book clutched to his chest, rain blurring the edges of the world. Then he turned, pulling his coat tighter, and slipped back into the city's veins.

The old station sat at the city's edge, half-forgotten, swallowed by vines and rust. It felt less like a place and more like a pause between worlds, where time itself had waited for permission to move again.

The glass roof sagged inward. The tracks vanished into weeds.

Neon from the skyline barely touched it, leaving the space bathed in an older kind of darkness.

Esra climbed the steps two at a time. And there, beneath the broken timetable board, sat Theo. Exactly as he remembered.

A weathered coat, waxed from time and storms.
A leather satchel, patched and overstuffed, resting like a sleeping dog beside him.
Long fingers wrapped around a chipped enamel mug. Steam still rose from it.
His face had aged, but not in the way that dims someone.

The lines were lived-in, not worn down. A streak of silver at his temples caught the platform light.
And those eyes, sharp, quiet, observant.
The kind that looked at you like a riddle, not a problem

"Well, look at you," Theo said, rising slowly, not with age, but the weight of waiting.
Not lost, just late. Or maybe . . . finally listening.

Esra didn't speak. Not yet.
He stepped forward. The rain pooled at their feet like the past collecting in puddles.

Theo opened his arms without a word.
Esra hesitated, then stepped in.
It wasn't long. Just enough to remember what safe felt like.

He thought of the dream.
The soft, pulsing light in the dark.
His mother's voice, the one memory he hadn't let anyone touch.
Not even now.

Theo tilted his head, not to intimidate, but to see something more clearly.

"There's a shift," he said. "Like something cracked . . . and now it can't be undone." He studied Esra's face. Not just the rain in his hair, or the weight in his shoulders—but something else.

"You've felt it for a while now. You just didn't know what to call it." Esra wondered if Theo saw it, the ache behind the questions. The need to be believed in. The kind of need no one says out loud. But almost everyone knows.

Esra said nothing. But he stepped closer.
Theo nodded, almost to himself.
"There it is," he whispered. "The boy with the dream."

His gaze dropped to the book. Not surprise, just . . . inevitability. "You opened it," he said. It wasn't a question.

Esra nodded.
"Good," Theo replied, voice low and certain.
"Then you're ready"

Esra stiffened.

Ready for what? A history? A prophecy? A mistake he couldn't undo.

He narrowed his eyes.
"What is this book, Theo? Why me?"
His voice echoed through the station, like it had been waiting for years to be asked.

Theo didn't flinch. He just smiled, like he'd heard this question a hundred times but had been waiting for Esra to ask it for himself.

He leaned back, a dry chuckle under his breath. "It's always that one. And always too soon."

He pointed toward the book with a nod.
A glint of mischief passed through his expression.
"Trust the questions. The answers have a habit of showing up when you stop chasing them."

"What does that even mean?" Esra muttered, tugging at his coat. Rain still dripped from his hair.
"I opened it. I saw what was inside, the history. The data. What more could there be?"

He looked down. Slowly opened the book again.
The pages were different now. Or maybe just waiting . . . for him to change.
There, in the center, etched as if by light itself, two words stood alone:

Time
Trains

Esra's breath caught.
He saw something shift in Theo's gaze, not surprise, but recognition, like a puzzle piece finally sliding home.

"Well," Theo murmured, sweeping his hand across the ruin and rust, "Seems we're exactly where we were meant to be."

He leaned in, elbows on his knees. "You've heard of the railways, haven't you?"

Esra gave a slow nod.
"Of course." Theo's voice dropped low. "Steel engines. Tracks that cut across entire nations."

But they didn't just carry passengers . . .

They carried a new way of living.

"Before the railways," he said, "time belonged to the sun."

Esra furrowed his brow. "Like . . . every town had its own time?"

Theo nodded. "Exactly. Each village set their clocks by its rising and falling . . . Midday in one town might be minutes, sometimes hours off from the next."

Esra listened.

The soft rain whispered through broken glass.
Each word travelled like smoke through centuries.
"But trains don't wait for sunsets," Theo said. "And wheels don't pause for village bells. They needed a time no sun could disrupt."

He moved his hands slowly sketching lines only he could see.
Esra tilted his head.
"And someone just . . . decided?" he asked, cautious.

"They could rewrite time?"
Theo nodded.

"They didn't just rewrite it, Esra. They standardized it."

Esra wanted to ask more, but part of him already knew the answer. Like the train had been running beneath his life for years, and he'd only just heard it whistle.

Clocks. Trains. Tracks.
And still, it kept circling back to data.
Why?

What was it trying to show him?

"What you know as Schedules. Departures. Arrivals, Esra. Mapped across nations. Printed. Memorized. Shared. Trusted."

Theo tapped the bench beside him. "All thanks to the Great Western Railway 1840. They demanded a single time across all lines."

"One heartbeat. One rhythm. An invisible law for a fractured land."

Esra shut his eyes for a beat. He could almost hear it: Steel on steel. Coal snapping in the dark. A hundred clocks giving up the fight. He opened his eyes again.

"Wait," he said. "You're saying . . . this wasn't just trains?"
Theo's gaze darkened. "It was much more."
A silence stretched between them. A chill danced down Esra's spine. It was starting to make sense . . . but it also didn't.

"So . . . time," he whispered, "was also data, in a way?"

Theo's eyes gleamed.
Esra sat back.

The station spun gently around him, shadows, rain, broken glass.
Questions pressed behind his ribs like held breath.
He looked up, voice tight.

"You're still not answering me. What is this book, some forgotten lesson? You talk trains and time like that's all there is . . . meanwhile I'm chasing shadows and riddles."

Esra gripped the book. It wasn't just a relic. It was unfolding inside him.

"This isn't just about history," he said, half to himself. "It's pulling at something else . . . something I can't name." Maybe this wasn't just about him.

He caught the flicker in Theo's eye.
"You're feeling it now," Theo murmured, almost reverently. "Not the facts. The weight behind them."

Esra hesitated. "And the dream?"
Theo tapped his chest again, just once.
"That feeling? Follow it. It's not wrong."

A pause.

Then Theo reached into his weathered coat and pulled out a slip of old paper.
Folded it once. Then again. And placed it in Esra's hand.
One word was scrawled across it:
Tulips.

Theo stood. His coat caught the wind like a torn sail on a ghost ship.
"If you want to understand where it all began to break," he said, voice already trailing into the storm, "Start with the flowers."

And just like that, he disappeared into the rain, leaving only the questions louder than before.

Tulips," he whispered aloud. The word meant nothing. And somehow . . . everything. The paper trembled in his palm, already soft from the rain.

He didn't know what it meant. But he knew this, nothing would be the same after today.

Sirens wailed. The world moved on. But something had shifted inside him.

A Soul Lost

*"The great danger of progress is that it leaves us empty
before we know it."*

— *Erich Fromm*

He stepped off the platform, not toward anything.
Just forward.

What was he supposed to see?
What did Theo want him to find?

He moved beneath steel beams and shattered skylights until he
reached the last café inside the station's crumbling shell, its roof
half-collapsed, screens flickering weakly against the dark.
One terminal still worked. Barely.

He typed in the word Theo had given him, Tulip.
The machine whirred like something waking from a long dream.
A flicker. A pause.

Rows of flowers bloomed across the fractured screen, vivid reds,
soft yellows, fields beneath a painted Dutch sky.

But then, beneath the petals: Tulip Crisis.
Esra leaned in, rain dripping from his hair. And the story spilled out.
Not steel or steam.
But flowers.

The Netherlands. 1630s.

Tulips, simple, delicate, captured hearts. But soon, it wasn't
beauty they traded.
It was madness.
A single bulb cost more than a house.
Promises fluttered through taverns, prices inked faster than
reason.

Misinformation spread like rot. And when the bubble burst, it wasn't just fortunes, it was trust that collapsed.

Data without truth is a mirror with no reflection.

A flutter overhead, wings catching air where no bird should be. Esra flinched. Looked up. Rusted rafters creaked; dust drifted through a crack in the ceiling.
Silence returned. Then, a faint click. A whirr. Another thread unfurled on the screen behind him.
He stood still, breath fogging faintly in the air.
Okay . . . now what? Trust the questions, Theo had said.
Easy for you to say, Esra thought. You're not the one standing here, chasing ghosts.

He glanced down at the book tucked against his side. It hummed faintly, like a heart remembering its rhythm.
He opened it. A soft glow rose from the page. Ink stirred. Shapes emerged.

Waves formed across the parchment. Tiny ships bobbed in ink-dark waters.
In the corner, a single phrase surfaced:

The South Sea Bubble. 1720.

He blinked. Boats shimmered, then faded into fog. The page turned blank again.
Esra turned back to the terminal.
Typed it in.

Promises of distant trade. Unimaginable riches.
Investors poured their lives into the South Sea Company, fueled by newspapers, rumours, and dreams.

Words printed faster than the truth could catch them.

When the wave broke, when truth clawed its way up,
The wreckage wasn't only measured in money, it was carved into people's lives.

Thousands were ruined. Silence crept across Europe like smoke after fire, smothering voices Esra would never hear. Information, once trusted, had been weaponized.

Esra stared at the screen, the glow washing across his face.

This wasn't just history. It was a warning loop. No one had been listening.

The machine gave a soft hum, a pulse in the stillness.
Esra's fingers hovered over the keys. The book stirred again.
He opened it.

A faint shimmer. Letters formed slowly, like breath held too long.

Gutenberg. 1440.

A press. A name. A key.
He typed it in. Printing Press.
And the world opened again.
Not with money.
Not with greed.
But with a gift.

Germany. 1440.

A man named Gutenberg carved letters into movable type, turning sacred, slumbering knowledge into rivers that would never sleep again.

Before him, stories hid in shadows.
Chained in halls only the powerful could enter. Only the privileged could touch.
Only the few could shape.

But now, words ran free.
The Gutenberg Bible wasn't just a book. It was a key.
Unlocking a thousand minds. Ten thousand dreams.

Esra closed his eyes. He could almost hear it,
the clatter of the press, ink pounding into paper, knowledge breaking loose into the world.

It wasn't just data anymore.
It was destiny.

But freedom casts shadows of its own.
The more knowledge spread; the more others tried to fence it in.

The screen dimmed. A final flicker. Then, stillness.
Esra looked down. The book in his hand pulsed faintly, warm against his palm.
He opened it.

Ink curled to life like breath on glass.
A date surfaced: **1710**. Then, curling script:

The Statute of Anne.

The first law to say: Ideas are worth something. Ideas can be owned.
His chest tightened.

In giving stories to everyone, had they also learned how to fence them?
The page turned on its own, softly, as if stirred by thought.
A name appeared:

John Graunt.

Plain. Unadorned. No titles.
No scholar. No prince.
A hat-maker.

But in 1604, he did what no king, merchant, or priest had done.
He gathered the dead.

Bills of mortality. Lists of the lost. And he listened.
He turned their silent passing into patterns. Into predictions.
Into protection, a map of survival.

The founder of demography, Esra realized. And I'd never even heard his name.

For the first time, data wasn't just memory.
It was foresight.

The book stilled in his hands. Ink faded beneath his fingertips.
Esra waited. Nothing came.
He stood, the stool scraping softly against broken tile.

The café had given him ghosts, enough to rattle something deep.
But not enough.

Michael Clark

What is all this leading to? What does any of it have to do with me . . . or her?
He stepped through the broken door.

Out into the old concourse. Rain tapped gently through a glassless ceiling, pooling in cracks, tracing steel rails swallowed by time.

He moved without urgency now.
Like someone being led.

The storm inside him had slowed his feet.
There had to be a reason for all this. There had to be.

They used data to prepare for plagues. For disasters. It wasn't cold numbers. It was life. It was breath. It was us.

Then, another thought. Sharp. Sudden.
He stopped. Clenched his fists.
My mother lost her job to a machine. She worked years, and for what? One upgrade, and they erased her like she was nothing.

And now I'm supposed to believe this book of riddles holds answers?

Rain slipped through fractured glass above, painting the station in blurred light.
He wandered past rusted benches and broken signs, until he reached the entrance.

The book warmed.
He paused.

Opened it.
This time, it wasn't names or charts.
It was motion.

A great wheel. Cogs turning. Machines breathing.
And behind them: numbers, not as meaning, but as measure.
As control.

The Industrial Revolution.

The shift from people to process.

From soul to speed.
Production over poetry. Efficiency over essence.
Is this what we traded her for?

He closed the book and held it to his chest
The past wasn't behind him.
It pulsed beneath his feet.
Data wasn't just history.

It wasn't just numbers.
It was memory.
It was identity.
It was life.

Fragmented. Repackaged. Resold. Forgotten.

Is this what happened to us?
Is this what happened to her?
And yet . . .

The book vibrated. A low, insistent hum.
He pulled out his battered phone. Its screen glowed faintly in the
dark. Punching the screen with a mix of fear and excitement.
It rang once.

Theo's voice answered, warm and steady, like memory.
"I knew you'd call again."
"The book's shown me so much," Esra whispered. "Wow, the
Industrial Age."

A pause. Then Theo's voice, soft as the rain:
"Little did we know, in chasing progress, we forgot what made us
human."

Esra closed his eyes.
He could hear it now, the hum of factories rising.
The clatter of endless machines.

"We thought faster was better," Theo said.
"We thought more was enough."
"But something got lost," Esra said quietly.

"Yes," Theo replied. "We stopped seeing the meaning behind the numbers.
We stopped seeing the people behind the work."

Esra pressed the phone tighter.
He didn't see factories anymore.
He saw faces.

"The world forgot that data once meant gift," Theo said.
"A way to remember. A way to care."

Esra looked out across the ruined tracks.
I lost it all, he thought. The photos. The music. The messages I wrote her. Gone. Just . . . gone.

Then aloud, "And instead," he whispered, "it became just . . . counting."

Rain deepened into a steady rhythm, washing the empty station in silver.

Theo's voice faded: "And it's only the beginning, Esra."

"But it doesn't have to stay that way." Esra whispered, "Where do I go now?"

Theo's voice returned, quiet, but firm: "Come to the library. There are some things you need to see with your own eyes."

Day We Lost Ourselves

*"You may know the name of a thing, but that
does not mean you understand it."*

— Richard Feynman

The library loomed like a forgotten cathedral, half-swallowed by the city's sleepless glow. Windows fractured. Stone walls bowed by time.

Esra hesitated at the threshold. Rain slid off his shoulders. Theo waited. No smile. Just a nod. They stepped inside. The hinges groaned, a sound like something remembering it was alive.

Inside: damp stone and paper. The lights barely worked, flickering like memory trying not to fade. A cracked terminal blinked. Theo gestured. Esra swiped his badge.

The cracked screen flashed a name. Not his.
A different face. Same shape, older edges. Eyes that didn't quite belong.
Esra frowned.
"That's not me."

A voice rasped through the speaker, tin-thin and tired.
"Probably a glitch. System's old. Records get crossed."
A pause.
"You're cleared. Go on in."

But Esra lingered, staring at the face, still and flickering, like it knew something he didn't.
Behind him, Theo was already walking, boots silent on the marble dust.
Deeper into the dark.

"What did you want me to see?" Esra called. Theo didn't stop. "History. But not the kind we write down.

The kind we forget." They stopped at a nondescript shelf. Theo pulled a worn book, thick and leather-bound.

"This one." Esra took it. Felt its strange weight. A key was tucked inside. Old. Iron. Heavy. Theo pointed past the darkened aisles.

Theo watched. Silent.
"What's this?" Esra asked.
"No more shortcuts," Theo said.

Then nodded toward the darkest corner of the library.
Past the collapsed shelves.
Past the broken elevators.

"Follow the iron rails," he said.
And then, without another word, he vanished into shadows once more.
Esra sighed.
"Why does he always do that?" he muttered.
"One day, he might actually say goodbye."

Esra clutched the book to his chest, the iron key warm in his palm. The library breathed around him.
He moved forward. Past cracked globes faded maps. A monitor overhead flickered to life.
Someone walking the opposite wing of the library.
Same coat. Same hair.

But the gait . . . wrong. Mechanical. Too certain.
Esra froze.
It was him. But not.
Another version. Another record.
Taken, copied, used.
The image glitched.

He swallowed and pressed on.
There, beneath the dust,
iron rails, barely visible, curved into the dark.

Michael Clark

Each step pulled him closer.
To something unseen.
Something waiting.

The rails ended at a heavy door, swallowed by shadow.
Above it, carved faintly in stone:
"To Remember, You Must First Unsee."

His heart thundered. He slid the key into the lock.
It turned with a groan, and the door opened. Not just books.
Screens. Fragments. Glimpses. Moment's thought lost, now
flickering back to life.
The door shut behind him.
A hollow thud.

The air pressed against his lungs, thick, heavy. Photographs
hung half-developed, music crackling from warped vinyl. Shelves
sagged under the weight of forgotten blueprints and brittle
scrolls. Dreams. Prayers. Warnings.

The book in Esra's hand pulsed, subtly, as if responding to
something in the room.
He moved forward.
On a cracked table, a reel of film lay coiled like a sleeping
serpent.

Without touching it, he heard it begin to hum.
A dusty projector, long dormant, sputtered to life.
On the far wall, an image flickered into being:

A silver plate. A man staring back.
Still. Silent. Captured.

"Daguerreotype," Esra murmured, the word arriving like a
memory from a place he'd never been.
The projector kept humming as though it knew there was more
to show.
He opened the book.

In response the film clicked again.
This time, movement.
People pouring from factories.

Mothers clutching children beneath gaslit skies.
Hope and smoke tangled in every frame.

Esra stepped closer.

He stared at the label:

1839. The Year We Captured Ourselves.

A chill crawled up his spine. This wasn't just history. It was the moment the world began watching itself.

A photograph.

The ancestor of the camera in his pocket.
He was staring at the birth of a habit he never questioned.

Esra stepped closer, something twisting in his chest.
Not fear. Not quite. Recognition, maybe.

For a moment, he thought he saw his mother's eyes in the crowd.
Not her. Couldn't be.
But the ache came anyway.

And then a flash of doubt.
Was he witnessing history?
Or was history . . . watching him?

He glanced behind, running his hand across a crumbling shelf.
"The more the world grew," he muttered,
"the smaller people became."

No longer souls full of stories.
Just names on paper.
Faces in frames.
Data points on someone else's map.

The book in his hands seemed to sigh, a faint glow bled into the air:

1860. Steel. Oil. Rail. Power.

Shadows spilled across the room. A desk emerged, cluttered with yellowed paperwork, receipts, deeds, oil maps.

Above it, dusty aged portraits, pinned to a crooked wall.
Carnegie. Rockefeller. Vanderbilt. Morgan.
Faces. Watching. Waiting.

The book whispered, "They didn't just build companies. They built empires. Out of what people needed to live, to move, to survive."

Esra stepped closer.
Oil contracts. Deeds. Telegraph records.
All stamped. Signed. Controlled.
They didn't just move goods.

They moved people.
They owned movement.
Owned time.
Owned progress.

Factories rose like forests of iron. Smoke laced the air like bruises.

And beneath it all, people moved like shadows, counted by the hour, priced by the pound.

"He'd seen versions of this before. But now . . . it felt personal."

Then a voice. Theo's voice, or maybe just the echo of it.

"We thought faster was better."
"We thought more was enough."

Esra flinched. Not from fear. From Anger.

He looked down at the book.
It pulsed. Demanding. Hungry.
His grip tightened.
What was this? A vision? A memory?
Was he getting closer to the truth, or further lost inside someone else's version of it?

The pages turned in his hands, as if driven by something unseen:

1876. The Voice Crossed Wire.

A sharp crackle filled the air.

A reel spun to life.
Alexander Graham Bell leaned toward a metal mouth,
"Mr. Watson, come here. I want to see you."

Esra didn't move.
His heart did.

A beat, then a drop. The first voice turned electric. A breath,
carried across wire.
He looked at the phone, the thing he trusted more than memory
itself.

But now . . . it felt distant.
What else have I taken for granted?
What else have I forgotten how to feel?

The book glowed. Data wasn't still anymore. It moved. It reached
for connection. It wanted to be seen.

Cities tangled in copper veins.
Laughter, grief, secrets, racing beneath the streets. The world
shrank. Esra felt it, faster, louder, but lonelier. Intimacy thinned.
Then came another pulse of light: 1901. The air carried our
stories, static. Music. Ghostly and faint, spilling from a wall
speaker. Radio.

By the 1920s, the sky was full of voices.
A billion words, floating above homes, drifting into dreams.

Not just connection. Influence. Presence. Power. Esra's breath
caught.
For the first time, we didn't just live beside data. We breathed it.

A rusted filing cabinet caught his eye, rusted with age, drawer
ajar. Something waited.

He pulled it open.
The metal shrieked like it hadn't been touched in years.
Inside, just one folder. Thick. Weathered. Marked with a name:
"ESRA" No surname.
No initials.
He opened it slowly.

Name: Esra
Surname: [—]
Age: 42
Role: Unverified
Citizenship: Unverified
Clearance Level: Unassigned
Status: Pending / Observed

The words bled uncertainty. Not him, but close enough to unsettle."
And yet, a photo was clipped to the inside. Grainy. Black and white. His face . . . aged.
Weathered.

A scar above the brow. Same eyes. But the spark behind them felt dulled.

As if something had been slowly erased.
He looked at his own hands.
Still young. Still his.

Beneath the paper, etched faintly into the folder's inner lining, symbols. Circular. Curved.

Almost . . . alive.
They shifted slightly as he moved. Not letters. Not numbers.
They looked like a language, but not one he knew.

For a moment, Esra didn't feel seen. He felt interpreted.
He closed the file.

His fingers trembled.
"This isn't just who I am," he whispered.
"but is it who I could become?"

Esra tightened his grip. The folder weighed more now, less like a record, more like a warning. A future he didn't choose. A version someone else drafted.

He placed it back, gently, like returning a ghost to its box.

The book in his arms stirred, warm against his chest.
The symbols on its spine shimmered again, a language rising to meet him.

But still unreadable.
Not yet.

He stepped into the library's stillness.

The door closed behind him, not with finality, but with intent.
Silence gathered like dust, thick in his lungs, settling over his thoughts.
He stood there, the book heavy in his arms, as if it carried not just stories, but everything he didn't yet have words for.

Seen enough?
The question surfaced in his mind, not Theo's voice, but his own.
Quiet. Unsteady.

He looked down. A fragile drawing on the floor. A crooked sun.
A red house.

The girl in yellow. Her again. He froze, breath snagging in his throat. The chalk lines glowed faintly in the half-light. Was this a sign?

A glitch? Hope trying to reach him?

Something caught in his throat. Amongst hope there was sorrow.
"We built tools to bring us closer," he whispered.

His voice cracked slightly. "But somewhere along the way . . . we stopped asking what it all meant," he murmured. "Or who we were becoming because of it."

He clutched the book tighter. It pulsed in his grip, not just a relic now. A reminder.

Data was changing," he whispered. Still staring at the drawing.
"But so were we. Quietly. Relentlessly."

Michael Clark

Silent Rewrite

"Those who tell the stories rule society."

— Plato

Esra stepped through the heavy doors of the library, the book warm in his arms. His chest was tight. The room still echoed in his mind.

Theo was waiting by the edge of the steps, coat buttoned to the neck, eyes scanning the street like he'd never really stopped watching.

"Come on," he said without turning. "Let's take a walk."

They moved in silence past shattered lamps and rain-dark stone. The city flickered with a tired glow. Overhead, a low mechanical hum stirred, methodical, insect-like.

A drone.

Esra's gaze lingered on it, unnerved. "They're always watching?" Theo didn't answer.

Finally, Esra spoke. "Those men . . . Rockefeller, Morgan, the rail barons. They didn't just build the world. They bent it."
His voice cracked slightly.

"They decided where people could live. What they could afford. Who got left behind."
Theo nodded. "And they made it feel normal."

They turned a corner. A billboard glitched mid-scroll, storm warning, shoes, celebrity scandal. Each frame vanished before it could settle, leaving only static in its wake.

Theo gestured to it. "That's not content. That's calibration."
Esra stopped walking.

"I saw it. The contracts. The deeds. But I didn't expect to feel it. I mean . . . " He broke off, rubbing his face.

"It wasn't history. It was . . . us. Today. Now."
Theo turned to face him.
"You want to know what makes a monopoly dangerous?"
Esra nodded, fists clenched.

Theo's eyes narrowed. "It's not control of goods. It's control of perception."
He stepped closer.
"They don't just sell to you. They tell you what's worth wanting."
Esra stared at him, stunned. "You mean . . . my feeds, my ads, even my choices . . . ?"
"Curated. Filtered. Reinforced."

Theo lowered his voice.
"And then, rewritten."

A screen flickered above them. Esra looked up. His own face, just for a second, ghosted across the glass. Then gone.

His blood ran cold.
"They're rewriting me?"
Theo nodded slowly.

For a moment, Esra thought of the folder in the cabinet.
The eyes in that photo.
His eyes, only dulled, hollowed, rewritten.
Should he tell Theo?
His grip tightened on the book.
Not yet.

"They don't delete you, Esra. They overwrite you. Layer by layer, until the original fades and even you can't remember what was real."

Esra stepped back, eyes wide. "That's insane."

"Is it?" Theo asked quietly. "Or is it just . . . subtle?"

Silence stretched. Then Esra's jaw tightened.

"No. No, this isn't right." His voice rose. "They don't get to decide who I am."

Theo studied him, like measuring something invisible.

"Good," he said.

Esra exhaled, trembling. "But how do I fight something I can't even see?"

Theo hesitated. When he spoke again, his voice carried a different weight, older now, and tired.

"Years ago," he said, "I worked for one of them. Helped build a system. One that sorted people, scored them, predicted their wants before they could voice them."

Esra blinked. "You?"

"I believed it would make things better," Theo said. "Fairer. Smarter. Safer."

He looked away. "Until I realized we weren't sorting data. We were silencing stories."

He took a breath.

"That's why I left. That's why I disappeared. And why I don't want you to."

Esra's face hardened. "Then what now? What do I do with this?"

Theo looked at the book in Esra's arms.

"You read. You question. You remember."

He paused.

"And when the time comes . . . you choose."

Another buzz passed overhead. Closer this time.

Theo's tone shifted, sharp now. Urgent.

"This conversation stays between us," he said. "If they know what you've seen . . . what you carry . . . "

He didn't finish.

Esra clutched the book tighter. It pulsed again, not just warm now, but alive. Like it could hear them.

His voice dropped.

"Why me?"

Theo stepped closer.
"Because you still feel something when the world goes quiet. And that means," he said, "you still know what's real and what is not."

A long silence passed between them.
Theo turned away.
"Go. Before they trace this."
Esra didn't move.

He clutched the book tighter. Its pulse answered his own, steady, alive.

Out on the street, the world kept humming, unaware, lost in his thoughts.
It's not just about her . . . is it? The dream. The book. The voice. They're showing me something. I just don't know what. Not yet.

"I'm not ready," Esra said, barely above a whisper.
Theo didn't turn back.
"Neither was I."
Then, just before he vanished into the mist, his voice came once more, softer this time:
"Stay human, Esra. We need you more than you know . . . "

Becoming Misunderstood

"The more data we collect, the less
we see the individual."

— Zeynep Tufekci

Esra stood frozen on the steps of the library, the silence stretching behind him like an unfinished sentence.

His breath curled into the cold air, chest still tight from everything Theo had said, or hadn't.

Somewhere in the distance, a garbage truck groaned to life. Daybreak. He blinked. He hadn't even thought about the time.

His badge dangled uselessly at his side, cracked, unreadable.

No pings. No messages. Just one missed call from his mother. With a friend, he texted. Be home soon.
The dream hadn't left him, it had simply changed rooms.

He turned toward the library's side entrance, pulled by something deeper than logic. The badge reader glowed red. Waiting.

Esra swiped.

ACCESS DENIED
He frowned and tried again.

ACCESS DENIED—UNRECOGNISED CREDENTIALS
He leaned in.
"I was here ten minutes ago," he whispered. "Don't you remember me?"

The screen glitched, static bleeding through.
Then . . . a face.
Not his.

Similar shape. Same eyes. But dulled. Hollow.
Less . . . him. His stomach dropped

It looked like someone who'd already been overwritten.

A voice crackled from the speaker, thinner than before, as if it had forgotten how to speak.

"System refresh in progress. Please wait for manual override."

Esra's jaw tightened.
"Wait? For who?"

No answer.
Then, a mechanical click. The lock disengaged.
The door creaked open by itself.

He hesitated. His hand drifted to the book in his pocket.
Theo's words echoed back: Stay human, Esra . . .

Esra stepped into the library's cold hush. No flickering consoles.
No hum of machines.
Just paper, dust, and time, breathing quietly.

He moved deeper into the stacks, drawn by instinct more than reason.
The book in his pocket began to thrum, faint at first, then stronger. Like it recognized something buried here.

He pulled it free. The cover was warm.
When he opened it, the page had changed.

1939.

A single number, inked like a secret.
He sat on a worn bench near the history aisle.
Letting the silence cradle him

Pages turned themselves in his mind: stock crashes, jazz, war.
He rubbed his temples, muttering aloud, barely above a whisper:
"The fall . . . "

A voice behind him replied,
Not startled. Not surprised. As if it had been waiting.

Michael Clark

"Digging into the fall, are we?"

He turned.
A woman stood between the shelves. Arms crossed. One brow arched.

She looked like she belonged to the building itself, a long coat dusted in parchment,
Hair braided with a streak of silver. A gold tooth glinted in the light when she smirked

Her voice, velvet and rust, folded into the quiet.
"I thought you might say it," she said. "The word. Most people never do."
Esra held the book tighter. "I didn't mean to. It just . . . slipped out."

"Ah." She stepped closer. "That's how it usually starts. Truth, slipping out through the cracks."

She tapped a dusty terminal beside her. Nothing. "Useless thing," she muttered.
Then to Esra, sharp again:
"What are you really looking for?
He hesitated. "Following a dream. Or maybe just an idea. I'm not sure anymore."

She tilted her head, studying him like a forgotten map.
"Some dreams don't care if you understand them," she said.
"They just need you to keep going."

He blinked. "That's comforting. I think."
"It shouldn't be."

Without another word, she reached into her coat
and slid a folded paper across the desk.

"For the next part," she said. "No small talk. No disclaimers. Just follow it."
By the time he looked up unfolding the paper, she was gone.
Not even the rustle of a footstep left behind.
Only silence.

Then . . .
A flicker of light above. Once. Twice.
A low hum underfoot.
And faint voices, not clear. But searching.

"Did someone say they saw him?

Esra froze. The air thickened. Silence turned sharp.
He moved. Fast. Ducking into a corridor, shadows stretching like
they meant to catch him. The shelves loomed, as if the books
were holding their breath.

At a desk, an open terminal. Esra unfolded the note. Handwritten
words:

1939. Lessons. Great. Depression.

He typed. Lines flickered across the screen:
The biggest economic collapse in U.S. history.
Could it have been avoided?

Missed payments. Failing banks. Slipping wages. The signals were
there. But no one put the pieces together. They had the data.
They just didn't look.

Esra stared at the screen. His chest tightened, not from fear, but
from recognition.
A knot rising in his gut, cold and insistent.
It wasn't the collapse that haunted him.

It was the silence before it. The slow, invisible unravelling no one
dared to name.
A whisper in his mind,
What else are we not seeing?

He pushed back from the desk; the scrape of his chair cracked
the silence like a rifle shot.

Shadows shifted. Lights buzzed again, stuttering.
Then: movement.
She stepped from the end of the aisle, backlit by a dying strip
of light.

The librarian.
Her silhouette shimmered like memory barely holding shape.
"You'll need this," she said, voice hushed but firm, urgent
as a pulse.
From her coat, she handed him an envelope, thick, sealed,
its edges yellowed with time.
"Don't open it until you're somewhere safe."

The moment her fingers left the envelope, the library seemed
to inhale.
Lights flickered, once, twice, then stilled, casting strange
shadows between the shelves

Somewhere deep in the stacks, a click echoed. Sharp. Mechanical.
And then, *A whisper, low and chilling:*

"Esra . . . "

He froze.
His name again, louder unmistakable. Not from her.
Another voice, closer now, cutting through the dark:

"He's here. Move."

Flashlights knifed between shelves, carving motion from stillness.
His grip tightened, the envelope slick in his clammy hands.
Every instinct screamed. Run.

He didn't think. He obeyed.
Boots slapping against the marble floor, each step a shot fired
through silence.
Dust and something electric clung to him, the scent of old
knowledge and something short-circuiting.
He raced through rows of books that blurred into motion. Light
flared behind him.

A door surged up ahead, steel-framed and shadow-lined. He hit
it hard, shoulder first, and burst into the street.

Cold air punched him in the lungs, sharp, metallic, alive. Rain
stung his skin. Neon bled across the pavement. The day had once
more turned to darkness.

The city hummed around him . . . watching.

He didn't look back. He couldn't.
The past, the present, and the possible future were chasing him now, and it didn't blink.

Measured and Forgotten

*"The things we measure are not necessarily
the things we value."*
—Tony Judt

Everything was too loud, too bright . . . too wrong.
Esra ducked into an alley and collapsed.
The city hadn't chased him, but something had followed. Not
footsteps. A feeling.

A wall slick with old water. Digital graffiti bleeding static. His
breath fractured in his throat.
Hands shook.
Then, he doubled over and vomited.

The sickness came from somewhere deeper than his stomach. A
truth, raw and rising, he couldn't name.
He wiped his mouth with a trembling sleeve.
What do they want?
What did I just see?

A security drone hovered above, blinked red, then veered off.
Esra slumped down, fingers curled around the envelope like
a lifeline.
The shadows didn't just hide him, they swallowed him. Rain
traced lines down his cheeks he didn't remember inviting.

The envelope felt older now in his young hands. Heavier. As if it
had always been meant for this moment.

He tore it open with shaking hands.
Inside, a single white card. Heavy stock. Three letters, pressed
into it like a code: GRP.

On the back: steady script, no flourish. Just certainty. Dr. Elise Morgan and a number.

Something stirred in him. Like a dream nearly remembered.

He pulled out his phone. One bar. Called.
Three rings. Then a voice, clear, calm, sharp:
"Yes?"

"I think . . . I think we're meant to meet. I don't know why. But, my name's Esra."
A pause. Then, soft recognition.
"You found the envelope."
His grip tightened.
"You were expecting me?"
"Not expecting," she said.
"But I knew someone would come."

Another pause.
"Did Theo send you?"
Esra blinked.
"You know Theo?"

"Enough to know what he doesn't say."

The line hummed. "Bring the card. And the book. Old district. Fourth gate. You'll know it when you see it."
Click.

The line went dead. He didn't think, he ran.
The streets narrowed with each turn. Asphalt gave way to stone. Neon dimmed. Time thinned.

And then, he saw it.
An iron gate. Rusted at the hinges. Sandstone walls cracked like dry skin.
In the center, a symbol. Not etched. Not carved. Raised. Faint. Familiar.

The seal from the envelope.
He touched it. The gate opened without resistance.
Gravel crunched beneath his steps.

Mist clung low to the ground. Moonlight spilled like half-forgotten thoughts.

At the end of the path, a structure. Modern. Angular. Cut from glass and steel.
Cold. Precise. Almost surgical. Yet something about it breathed.
The door stood wide.

And at its threshold, she waited.
Dr. Elise Morgan didn't move. She didn't need to.
Coat caught in the wind like a second skin. Still. Sharp-eyed.
Not unkind.

She didn't speak. Instead, she turned.
And walked inside.
Esra followed. An invitation without words.
The glass whispered shut behind him.

Inside: soft echoes. Clinical light. Whiteboards scrawled with formulas. Projection glass flickering.
Silence, thick as thought.

She waited at a desk cluttered with journals. Her eyes, like flint, held him.
"Esra," she said. Not a question.
He nodded. "Yes."

She gestured to the table between them.
"Put it down."
He placed the envelope. The card slid free. GRP, faintly pulsing.
Dr. Morgan didn't touch it. Instead, she handed him a folder.
"Start here," she said. "You'll have questions."

Then she left the room.
He opened the folder slowly.
Not just a report, a relic.
Near the back, a clipped article scanned from an economic journal.

SIMON KUZNETS: THE ARCHITECT OF GRP

GRP. Gross Regional Product. A way to score a region, by how much it made, sold, and spent. But it never counted what really mattered.

Kuznets didn't just measure economies. He gave us a lens. A new way to see the world. And it changed what we noticed, and what we didn't.

Esra frowned.

A lens? What did that even mean?

What seemed like eternity passed, then, footsteps. She returned.

"You're not meant to get it all at once," she said, gently.

"That sentence . . . it's not about numbers. It's about value, Esra."

"Value we chose to see, and value we chose to ignore."

He looked up, unsure.

"Why would we ignore value?"

Her eyes softened. "Because it made the world easier."

She tapped a screen beside them. A city street, blurred with motion.

"But once you only measure what you can count," she said, "everything else begins to disappear."

Then her tone changed. Sharpened.

"Where did you get the envelope?"

Esra looked up. Her voice wasn't harsh, but something firmer threaded through.

Curiosity edged with concern.

"It was given to me," he said. "In a library. I got there because of this."

He lifted the book. "This guided me. With Theo."

Her posture stiffened, just slightly. The way someone braces when they see something they thought was lost or never expected to return.

"Where did you get that?" she asked, barely above a whisper.

And Esra told her.

About his mother.
The dream.
The silence.
The bookstore.

The weight he couldn't explain. Like carrying something invisible.
Something pulling him forward, toward a place he hadn't known
existed . . . until now.

When he finished, the room held its breath.
Even the lights hummed quieter.
She didn't speak for a long time.

Her fingers grazed the table, a gesture too slow to be casual.
Something flickered in her eyes.
Then . . . calmly:
"You're on the right track." She turned back to the file.

"GRP was a breakthrough. But it also did something else."
"It turned the world into a balance sheet."

Esra frowned. "A balance sheet?"

"Before GRP," she said, "value wasn't just numbers. It was family.
Community. Meaning."
She drew a line across the desk.
"But when we reduced everything to money,
what couldn't be counted slowly disappeared."

She tapped a screen on her desk.
A grainy image appeared, a city street blurred with motion.
People, data, decisions, all reduced to a moving pattern.
"Behind every number is a life," she whispered. "But the balance
sheet doesn't see that."
Esra leaned closer.

"So, GRP told us what we produced . . . but not what made life
worth living?"
"Exactly."
Her voice hardened.
"It showed how much, but never why.

GRP gave us structure. But that system narrowed our sight.
It taught us to value productivity over people. Outputs over
understanding. Efficiency over meaning."

Dr. Morgan glanced toward a wall of dusty binders stacked
like tombstones.
"And so," she continued, "people, real people, started to
disappear from the equations."
Esra's breath caught.

A memory, sharp and uninvited, rushed in—
his mother's voice on the phone. Muted. Cracked.
She too disappeared from the equation . . .
Is this why I'm here? Is this why me?

She continued, quieter now:
"Most leaders became little more than accountants.
And data, our greatest gift, its true value never recorded. Lost."

Each word landed like a pebble falling into a deep well inside him.
"We stopped asking why," she said.
"We only measured how much."

Then, as if remembering something too old to hold gently, she
added, "And soon, a crisis came."

"What crisis?" he asked.
Dr. Morgan smiled, slowly.
The kind of smile that says you're close. But not there yet.
"Patience, my friend," she said.
"Find it yourself. When you do, we'll talk again."

She turned back to her work.
Esra sat still.

It was too much. The truths, the memories, the weight of it all, it
washed through him like a tide.
Something inside him had shifted.
He didn't yet know what, only that it wouldn't shift back.
Then, silently, he stood, walked out into the night,
and didn't look back.

10
Rebuilding and a Die is Cast

"In the rush to rebuild and move forward, we often forget to ask: progress toward what, and at what cost?"

— Michael Clark

The city had moved on. Esra hadn't.
Months since the library. Since Morgan's truths and Theo's warnings cracked his mind open.

The search lights were gone now. Drones still passed overhead, but they no longer searched for him.
Not openly.

His name had cooled, like old code, still flagged, but not pursued. Most nights he walked—not to hide, but to feel something. The rain. The pulse of the grid. The friction between forgetting and remembering.

And tonight, something was different.
The book stirred, a low thrum beneath his ribs.
It had been silent for weeks.
Now it matched his heartbeat.

What was the crisis? he thought.
Why did no one speak of it?

The book grew warmer. A dull glow pushed against his jacket lining.
It was leading him.

Across the street, a low hum split the air.
Esra froze.

A drone scanned the street, silent, slicing rain with light.
The drone paused mid-sweep. As if the air had changed. As if something had turned it back on.

Esra ducked behind a battered kiosk. The glow from his coat pulsed harder.
Awake again. After all this time, but why now?

He pressed a palm to his chest.
The warmth had rhythm.
Like a heartbeat not his own.

As the drone drifted past, Esra emerged from the shadows. The book tugged, not outward, but inward. Toward the Civic Archive Building.

He'd passed it a hundred times, but tonight, it whispered like a memory.

He stepped through the archive doors as the rain quieted behind him. As he passed under the dim, sensor-lined archway, the glow intensified.

He pulled the book from his coat, the cover pulsed once, then the page turned itself.
A single number etched in faint ink:

1937.

Not a whisper or command, a memory. A direction.
Inside, the air smelled of old circuits and older dreams.

He walked past a row of terminals. Most were dark. One blinked, waiting.
He placed his hand on it.

"Welcome," a voice chimed, cold and procedural.
"Please confirm user credentials."

Will they trace me, will my identity even work?

A pause.
Before he could turn away, he noticed the station next to his.
Still lit. Unlocked.
Someone had left in a hurry.

He hesitated, then slid into the vacant seat.
"Input?" the machine asked.
He whispered, "Nineteen thirty-seven."

The screen flickered.
Data. Identity. Technology.
And then it appeared, a flicker in the timeline, a name he didn't recognize:

George Stibitz.

In a kitchen lit by a single overhead bulb, a man soldered wire.

The Model K. A machine capable of simple arithmetic.
Nothing extraordinary. Not at first glance.

But it was. It was the spark. A new pulse had entered the world.
Esra leaned in, reading faster now. The machine hadn't been built for war.
It hadn't been built for conquest.
It had been built to help.

To augment humanity.
And somehow, in the glow of the archive screen, he felt
the fracture.
What was meant to free us had become something else.
War.

The word struck him like lightning.
This was it. This must be the crisis.
But just as his hand moved to call Theo, something stopped him.

At the far end of the hall, someone was crying.
Soft. Broken. The kind of sound that didn't belong in a place
of silence.
A woman, early fifties, maybe, sat beside a blank terminal,
clutching a chipped identity card.

Her hands trembled.
"I've come three times," she whispered. "They said it would be
fixed. That it was just a glitch."

Esra stepped closer. "Are you okay?"
She looked up, eyes red. "I used to be someone," she said. "I
wrote music. Played all over the city. Now the system says I never
existed."

She held up a faded data tag. "They erased me. Even the credits on my songs. Gone."

Before Esra could respond, a voice snapped through the hall. "Marla."

A man approached, archive staff. Tired. Clipboard under his arm. "I've told you before," he said. "You can't keep coming back here."
"I just want to prove . . . "

"There's nothing we can do."
She closed her hand around the tag. Folded inward.

"I'm sorry," she whispered to Esra. And walked out.

He froze. Not in pity, in recognition.
How many others had been erased?
How many stories undone, not by war or time, but by systems built to forget?
And for the first time in months, the ache from his dream returned.
Not his mother, something more. Something larger.

He pressed call.
The line clicked.
"Theo."
A beat of silence.

"I found it. Dr. Morgan's crisis."
His voice was low. Almost reverent.
He exhaled, the words catching in his throat.
"The fracture. The moment it all began to bend."

"We need to meet," Theo said. "But not alone. Dr. Morgan should be there too."
What you're about to uncover . . . it's been buried for decades. You ready?
Esra nodded into the silence. "Yes."
Click. The line went dead.
Dr. Morgan's building loomed beneath the weight of a storm-smeared sky.

When Esra arrived, Theo pulled him in from the shadows, eyes scanning, breath tight, like the air might betray them.

Inside, the noise of the city fell away.
Dr. Morgan stood waiting.
She looked at Theo first, not surprised, but resolved.
"Good," she said quietly. "You're both here."
Then her eyes settled on Esra.
"I had a feeling it wouldn't take you long." she said. The door whispered shut behind them.

"Was it war?" Esra asked.
"Is this the crisis?" Theo nodded.
So did Dr. Morgan.

"But it's not that simple," she said.
"To understand the crisis," Theo added, "you have to understand the desperation."
They began to weave it together.

As war swept across continents, nations fought not just for victory, but for control.
"Identity became currency," Dr. Morgan said.
"More valuable than gold."
"Cards. Passes. Registries," Theo echoed.

"Who you could prove you were . . . meant the difference between safety and disappearance." Esra felt the words settle in his chest.

She then tapped a panel.
1944. MIT. A failed flight simulator project. "But out of it," she said, "came the first working memory system." Theo stepped forward.

Theo stepped in. "ENIAC, 1946. A room-sized machine meant for artillery, but it changed everything."

"It wasn't just war," Dr. Morgan said. "It was rebirth."

"And from that rebirth," Theo added, "came the world we now live in."
But they weren't done.

"After the war," Dr. Morgan continued, "came recovery. Trade. Alliances. And something new . . . accounting."

She touched the screen again.
A pale glow illuminated three letters: SDR.

"Special Drawing Rights," she explained.
"Not currency. Not loans. Just a consensus of value. Created in 1969 and unanchored from anything real. Value no longer walked on ground—it floated in belief.

Esra tilted his head.
"So . . . we just decided it was worth something?"

Theo nodded.
"Exactly. That's when value stopped being real.
It became . . . myth."

Esra frowned.
"You mean . . . stories about money?"
Dr. Morgan met his gaze. "Stories that made numbers feel real. Numbers we trusted, even when they meant nothing."
Theo leaned in. "Like . . . GDP?"

Esra blinked.
"GDP?"

He frowned deeper. "I've seen it on TV. But I never really knew what it meant."
She looked at him, almost warmly.
"Gross Domestic Product. We focused inward. Measured output, not meaning."

Theo's voice lowered.
"We built an economy on velocity, not wellbeing.
Speed. Over soul.

Esra sat back, his thoughts spiralling.
SDRs. GDP. Control masked as stability.

And at the center, always, was data.
Dr. Morgan leaned forward.

"Data wasn't the enemy. But how we treated it, that changed everything."

"We taught machines to remember us," Theo said.
"But not to understand us." Dr. Morgan tapped again.

"And then we taught people to forget."

The room dimmed.
Three fracture points appeared in sequence to many they were missed, harmless.
Data defined as statistics in the dictionary.
Identity reduced to a mainframe password for the first time.
Value bound to mass production.
The trident broken. Quietly. Permanently.

Esra stared at the screen.
"So . . . " he whispered, "the bond between who we are, the data we create and value . . . started to fall apart?"
"Exactly," Dr. Morgan said.
"And that crack . . . is still widening."

A new image glowed.
Test sheets. Clock towers. Rows of steel bells.
"Education became focused on getting a job", she said.
"We stopped raising thinkers. We started manufacturing workers."
"And most children," Theo added, "even today don't know their history."
For them history does not go beyond the industrial Age, because that's where the story ends."

"Don't believe me, ask a 14-year-old who Nelson Mandela was. Expect silence."
"Because the next chapters," Dr. Morgan said, "were never written for them."

Esra sat still.
Inside him, the pieces clicked.
Data. Identity. Value. Education. Industry.
The great crisis wasn't one explosion. It was erosion.

A long chain of choices, small at first, then catastrophic.
The ground had shifted, and no one noticed.

Theo broke the silence. "Now you know."
He turned toward the window, toward a city still spinning its illusions.

"But don't expect it to listen." And then, he was gone.

Dr. Morgan didn't look up.
"When the next page turns, Esra . . . it won't be just you turning it."

He wasn't chasing the past anymore. He was carrying it.
And maybe, just maybe . . . he was beginning to understand why.

The book hummed.
Somewhere in the distance, a system pinged. A location locked.
A signal sent.
Esra didn't see it.
But someone, or something did.

11
Balance Sheet Mentality

"A fool knows the price of everything and the value of nothing."

— *Oscar Wilde*

The book sat heavy under Esra's arm, a silent weight against his ribs. Its pages still whispered, still hummed, but it offered no more answers tonight.

Across the room, Dr. Morgan watched him. "You're beginning to see it," she said quietly. "The way the pieces fit."

She gestured for him to sit, her voice low and urgent. "We talked about balance sheets," she said, "but I need to show you what that mentality did, not just to economies, but to people. This isn't theory anymore, Esra. It's personal."

She tapped the screen. Images flickered, old ledgers, brittle balance sheets, currencies faded by time. "After the war, the world needed order. Standards. Rules. And balance sheets became the framework, not just for companies, but for everything."

Esra frowned. "Balance sheet mentality?"
She nodded. "The idea that everything, even people could be measured. A line item. An expense. A resource."

She leaned back. "It made rebuilding easier. Numbers made decisions cleaner. Profits. Losses. Output. Nothing else."

Esra stared at the glowing screen, the data washing coldly across his face. "And people?"
"Just another number," she said. "Salaries. Overheads. Redundancies. If you cost more or if there was a cheaper way to do it, you disappeared from the story."

He leaned back, tension clawing behind his ribs. The absence of humanity hidden behind arithmetic.

His voice cracked, "That's how the world still sees us, isn't it?" Dr. Morgan nodded. "It's why the world feels so hollow. We stopped asking what makes life valuable. We only count what makes it profitable."

He turned away, swallowing the ache rising in his throat.
That's why she lost her job. His mother.
Not because she wasn't good enough. But because a machine could do it faster. Cheaper. No questions. No soul.

He remembered the stories, how she helped people. Her hum as she worked. How what she knew touched so many. The look on her face the day of the phone call. How she changed.
She wasn't inefficient. She was unaccounted for. Just another cost to be cut.

The screen beside them dimmed. Dr. Morgan leaned forward. "There's more. The next phase, the 1970s, added layers. Debt. Trade. New systems on top of old ones. Painted over. Never healed."

She opened a drawer and slid a slim folder across the desk. "This isn't your path," she said. "The book will show you that. But this . . . this is a flashlight for the darkness ahead."

Esra tucked it into his coat. The paper scraped his skin, colder than it should have been.
Then, outside, a sound. A mechanical buzz. Faint but rising. The lights in the room flickered.

Dr. Morgan stiffened. "They've found you." A shadow pulsed across the glass . . . drone sweep. Esra moved quickly. No words. No goodbye. Down the back stairwell, into the street.

The rain was back. The air smelled of oil and ozone. Neon blurred in puddles. The hum of rotors passed low overhead. He darted through alleyways, winding deeper into the city's underbelly. The folder pressed to his chest, the book tight under his arm.

Eventually, the lights faded. The hum receded. He exhaled.
And nearly collided with a figure standing beneath a lamppost.
The man was still. Watching. Like he'd been waiting all night.
"You're the one digging into the past, aren't you?" Esra froze,
clutching the folder tighter. "Excuse me?"

The man shrugged; his smile half-formed. "The great crisis. The
broken world. All that. Sounds like a lot of chasing ghosts."

"And you are?"

"Call me Simon," the man said, like the name didn't matter, like
he'd worn many. He nodded toward the folder. "I hear things.
And what I'm hearing . . . is that you're wasting your time."

"If it's all meaningless," Esra said, "then why are you here?"

Simon's smirk didn't reach his eyes. "Maybe I'm just curious. Or
maybe I've seen this story before. Always ends the same."

He stepped closer. No emotion. "The world doesn't need
fixing . . . it's running exactly as designed."

Esra shook his head. "No. It's broken. And understanding how it
broke, maybe that's how we evolve it."

Simon tilted his head, studying him like a crack waiting to widen.
"Or maybe it's always been broken. And all you'll find are more
cracks." The words struck harder than expected.

Doubt rose again, cold, sharp. Was he chasing shadows?
Simon saw it. And smiled. "Suit yourself," he said, turning into
the mist. "But don't say I didn't warn you . . . when it all falls apart."

And then he was gone. Swallowed by the dark. The folder
trembled in Esra's hands. And for the first time, he felt it. Not just
the cost. The loss. The forgetting. He looked down at the book.
And whispered into the rain, "Not anymore."

Auction of the Unseen

"In the end, we will not be defined by what we created,
but by what we chose to value."

— Anonymous

He walked through the half-waking city, its lights flickering like memories trying to return.
"Not anymore," he'd said. And he meant it. No more forgetting. No more looking away.

The folder thudded like a second heart, heavy with meaning he hadn't yet faced. The book under his arm, alive with stories that refused to be buried.

He didn't know exactly what he was looking for, only that he had to keep looking.

Rain kissed the rooftops. Cables stitched the city like old scars. The fog lingered between buildings, making everything feel dreamt, half-formed. like a memory you almost remember, but never fully do.

Then, like something called to him through the mist, he found it.

Tucked between two fractured towers: The Last Cup

Its sign hung crooked, metal chains rusted, the letters faded like forgotten names. Inside, the booths were slouched with age. One radio fought through static, a love song barely alive.

An old man slept in the corner, or maybe he was part of the furniture now.
Esra sat alone. Dust curled in the light, and the window beside him glowed faintly with dawn.

The folder fell open with a whisper.

Yellowed clippings. Scrawled notes. A headline caught his eye, "Scientists Send First Message Over ARPANET."

He read slowly.
UCLA to Stanford. A simple message: LOGIN. But the system crashed after just two letters. L.O.
Esra paused.

Even in failure, the world had changed.
A signal had crossed the silence.
Connection had begun.
Next to the clipping, a note in Dr. Morgan's hand,
"What began as a military tool planted the seeds of today's networks. But even then, we didn't grasp what we were unleashing."

We built the machines.
But not the meaning.

Then came a heavier page, not in weight, but in consequence.
"Nixon Ends Gold Standard, Dollar Floats Free."

Esra frowned under the café's dim light.
This was the moment the world let go of something real.

The last tether, the gold standard snapped.
From that day on, money wasn't tied to gold or grain or anything you could hold in your hand.

It floated on trust. On belief. On the illusion of value.
It was meant to save the system. But something deeper broke.

He could almost hear Dr. Morgan's voice, steady and precise,
"This is where the balance sheet mentality dug in deeper. We removed the anchor but kept the same map.

Money became an idea, but we kept acting like it was still metal and weight and labour. We entered an intangible world . . .
And tried to measure it with rulers made for bricks and bolts."

We changed the rules of reality, he thought. But not the way we measure it. And we've been lost ever since.

Outside, the fog was thinning. Neon signs blinked against glass like old memories trying to return.

Esra stepped out into the street, the folder tucked under his jacket.
A digital billboard flickered above him, an AI ad selling the ideal life no one really lived.

A woman and child laughing in soft-focus sunlight—a loop too perfect to be real.
Polished for strangers. A memory that never was.

But something about it caught him, the tilt of the woman's head. The way the child reached up.

His breath caught. Just for a second . . . it looked like her.
Back when things felt whole.
He had to remember. Had to see her.
He unlocked his phone, fingers moving before thought.
An old app. A social platform from before everything splintered.

Login failed. Forgotten password. Reset link, gone. So was the account.
He opened a browser. Dug deeper. Searched his name.
The screen flooded, names, links, leaks, versions. Too many. And still . . . none of them were him.

He clicked one.
"Contact not found. Last message, 'Dad, please just call me.'"
His voice, not his message.

Another link. A broken video file. Three seconds. A girl singing. It cut off mid-note.
Filename: Untitled_421_finalfinal.mp4.
He didn't know the girl, but the ache in her note felt like it remembered him.

One more profile surfaced. Empty, except for a thread long corrupted. Only one line remained, "You promised you wouldn't disappear again."

His thumb hovered over the "Request Deletion" button.
The screen blinked. Waiting.
Which parts are fake? he thought. Which are real?
If I delete everything . . . do I erase what mattered, too?

He backed out.
Not yet.

He stood in the grey morning, phone in hand, still feeling
the weight of the choice he hadn't made.
The city buzzed with signals and yet, he couldn't find
himself. Or her.
His jaw tightened. They broke the story, his life, into so many
pieces, he could no longer remember what it was supposed to
say.

He looked up at the blinking lights. The silent systems. The
scaffolding of someone else's design.

"Can we change this?" he whispered.
Or are we too far gone?
Not to anyone. Just . . . out loud. To the fog. To the ghosts.
To himself.
As if listening, the book beneath his arm pulsed, a single, steady
warmth against his ribs.
Alive. Present. Waiting.

A sudden chill traced the back of his neck. He looked up.
Across the street, half-hidden by the curling fog, a sign swung
lazily in the breeze: Tech Repair Data Recovery Electronics
Bought and Sold.

The windows were cracked. The paint was peeling. The neon
letters flickered and buzzed, spelling nothing in particular. The
store looked abandoned. Forgotten.
Or maybe . . . maybe it was waiting too.

He stepped into the fog-draped street. The book, warm in his
grip. The folder, a question pulsing against his chest. This time,
he wouldn't just carry the past, he'd press against it, see what
pushed back.

Michael Clark

13
Fragments: Power and Possibility

"Humanity's greatest power lies not in what we have built, but in what we are yet to imagine."

— Anonymous

The door creaked.
The tech shop breathed dust, pulsing with the hum of forgotten things.

Screens covered the walls, cracked like old phone glass. Some flickered softly, like they hadn't realized the world had moved on. Circuit boards spilled out of boxes. Sticky notes still clung to keyboards like someone meant to come back.

Behind the counter, the old man leaned over a machine, thick goggles strapped to his face.
He muttered to it like it might wake up if he said the right thing.

"You're late," he said, not looking up. "Real memories are harder to come by these days. But hey, you didn't step on the cat, so you're already better than most."

Esra blinked, confused. "I think . . . you're supposed to help me?"

The old man finally looked. Grinned. "Looking for a cursed music player? Or maybe a fax machine that only prints 'I miss you' messages from 1998?

Esra shook his head. "I'm not here to buy. I think you know something."

The Merchant paused. His eyes were too bright for someone living in so much shadow. He glanced at the book and folder in Esra's hand. Something shifted.

He reached out slowly, fingertips brushing the folder like it might dissolve.
"You kept it alive," he whispered.

He opened it. The paper felt warm, like it had been holding its breath.
A date leapt off the page, 1970s.

At the top, in messy handwriting:
"This is a story no one ever told you."
Esra's breath caught. His fingers hovered above the page like it might shatter.
The room felt still, like it was listening.
He wasn't just reading history.
He was walking into it.

The Merchant ducked beneath the counter. When he came back up, he was holding something the size of a shoebox.

Wires dangled from the side. A single light blinked, slow, unsure.
"This," he said quietly, "was the dream. A computer in every home. Something you could plug into the wall, and suddenly, you were part of the future."

He set it down like it was sacred. Then pointed to another. Sleeker. Heavier. Curved like it wanted to be something.

"This one," he said, with a half-smile, "thought differently."

He didn't name it. He didn't have to.

"Hardware and software built together. It was beautiful. But even then, even at the beginning, something was missing."

The Merchant stepped back, arms folded.
"They didn't build it to connect," he said. "They built it to compete. To win."

He pointed to a cracked screen behind him, its glass spidered with age.
"See that? That's what's left when companies race to sell the next machine, but never stop to ask, How do we make them talk to each other?"

Esra turned, scanning the shelves.
Piles of old tech.
Laptops with missing keys.
Phones that hadn't lit up in years.
Stacks of CDs.
Wires tangled like seaweed.
Monitors blinking faintly, trying to remember who they used
to be.

"If they'd built for connection," the Merchant said softly, "half this
place wouldn't exist."

He swept his hand across the cluttered room.

The folder in Esra's hands grew heavier. The pages flicked past:
Operating systems.
Icons.

A world moving from lines of code to clicks and swipes.
"They made it easier. Faster. Cleaner," the Merchant said. "But no
one asked, what happens to the data underneath?"

"They called it a revolution.
But really, it was a race.
A sprint to flood the world with devices.
Then, almost without noticing, software ruled everything.
Data everywhere, yes.
But software was king.
Data? Just an afterthought."

He looked up, jaw tight.
The Merchant was watching.
"They built software to dazzle. To dominate.
Not to connect.
Not to care who might be left behind, or where the data went."
He gestured to Esra. "Don't believe me? Look for yourself."

Esra pulled out his phone. The dust in the air caught the light as
he looked down.
He wasn't searching for her.
He just wanted to see if anything still made sense.

Contacts, half-synced. Names scrambled.
Notes, dated wrong. Some showing up from the future.
Photos, duplicates, wrong timestamps, saved in apps he hadn't opened in years.

His phone was full. But empty. A thousand memories, scattered, scrambled, forgotten.
The breadcrumbs of who he was.
Just scattered traces, like someone had erased the lines between his past and present.

This wasn't just data.
It was him.
And no one had cared to keep it whole.
No clear picture of who he was.

He walked over to a strange, hulking machine in the corner—parts of it taped together, others rusted and glowing faintly.

"That one?" he said. "Built from ten different systems. Ten different decades.
Someone tried to make them talk. It never really worked. But sometimes, when it hums, it remembers."

Esra blinked. The dust in the air was thick now, and his chest was tight. All this time, he'd been chasing answers.

But here, in this half-lit graveyard of machines, it didn't feel like history anymore. It felt like a mirror.
And in it, he wasn't sure he liked what he saw.

"They didn't see data as the treasure," the Merchant said quietly. "They saw it as background noise.
Disposable.
So it scattered and so did we."

Esra looked again at the old devices . . . once magical, now abandoned.
It wasn't a junkyard. It was a graveyard of what could have been.

The rise of the companies he'd grown up admiring suddenly felt . . . different.

Less like a triumph.
More like a warning.

He turned the page.
One line stared back at him in red ink, Dr. Morgan's handwriting sharp and fast:
What if we had gotten it right?
What if data had been the most important thing, from the start?

Esra stared.
He imagined a world where every photo, every message, every memory lived together, not trapped in silos, but moving with him.
A world where systems spoke.
Where data wasn't lost but lived.

And then it hit him.
This wasn't just a lesson.
This was part of his dream.

He closed his eyes, and her voice flickered,
like a laugh pulled from a corrupted file.
He reached for it.
Gone. Only silence. And the ache it left behind.
"It would've been different," he whispered. "Better . . . maybe."

The Merchant nodded.
"Maybe. Or maybe it had to crack, so someone like you could see what's underneath."

Esra looked again at the wreckage,
not as failures,
but as signals.
Coordinates.

Open doors left ajar,
for a boy with a dream.

A knot twisted in his stomach.
What if it couldn't be fixed?
What if it was already too late?

He didn't feel chosen.
He felt behind. Like someone waking up mid-game, holding pieces to rules no one ever wrote down. The cracks wouldn't wait. They'd spread, with or without him.

Esra stepped back from the folder, heart thudding.
The book in his pocket pulsed, warm, alive, as if it knew.
He reached for it, fingers brushing the spine like it might vanish.
And he understood.

Each page wasn't just a way to see the world.
It rewrote the world he thought he knew.
Not just stories.
But history, lived, lost, blindly repeated.

"They weren't villains," the Merchant said.
"Just builders, chasing innovation, not silence.
Dreaming in code. But never stopping to ask what was buried beneath.
The tools dazzled.
But they disconnected."

He turned, eyes scanning the shelves of fractured machines.

"And the world they left us?
Siloed. Fragmented. Full of echoes and broken timestamps.
Not by design, but by inheritance.

They carried the baggage of the past into the future . . .
And called it progress."

We thought they built the future. But really, they lit the spark and no one watched where the fire went.

They didn't know the ground was cracked, or that they were laying foundations on fault lines.

All this time, Esra thought he was chasing a dream.
A new path.
But really,
he'd been walking through the fractures of someone else's past.
And now? It was his turn to connect the pieces.

Michael Clark

A pause.
His phone buzzed.
Pulled him back.

New message.
No name.
You're close.
I will find you.
Three dots. Typing . . .
Then nothing.
Just silence.

Who, or what, might be searching for him?
And whatever it was . . .
it wasn't waiting for permission.

14
Echoes of a Broken Web

"What if the machine was never meant to replace us,
but to remind us what we forgot."

— The Merchant

The message blinked away.
Silence returned, but not peace.
Esra stared at the phone. His hand trembled.
"You're close."

The words echoed louder than the silence they left behind.

From the shadows, the Merchant was already watching, eyes
glinting like glass marbles lost in time.
"Some things," he said, voice worn and strange, "are best
remembered . . . not searched for."

He turned, coat sweeping like a curtain drawn between
dimensions.
And with that, the room began to shift.

Esra tightened the strap around the battered folder, the book still
cradled beneath his arm, but something tugged at him.

A weight that hadn't been there before. A corner slipped free.
A slip of paper drifted down like an old secret trying to escape.

He bent to pick it up.
Hastily inked, edges curled:

1991. The World Wide Web is born.

When he rose,
the Merchant was already watching, eyes sharp, lit from within.
"Not here," he rasped. "Some pages prefer the dark."

He moved toward a dented metal door tucked behind the counter. The door responded with a low, mechanical hum, not a welcome, but a warning.

The air shifted as he crossed the threshold. Colder. Denser. Alive. Inside:
the light dimmed, not by switch, but by intent.

It was a room that didn't like being seen.
Objects filled the space like memories left out to rust.

Hollow-eyed devices stared from shelves lined in velvet and dust. Plastic limbs from forgotten robots lay next to reels of warped cassette tapes.
A cracked VR headset blinked once, as if dreaming something it could no longer render.
An early voice assistant, still waiting to be asked something meaningful.
Everything here had once promised the future,
and then been quietly buried by it.

One screen flickered on. No cable attached. Just static and a whisper:
"You left me."
Esra's breath hitched. He wasn't alone.

The room wasn't just full of objects.
It was full of echoes.

The Merchant tapped a table in the center of the room with one knuckle, the sound sharp in the thick air.

"1991," he said quietly. "The year everything changed."

Esra moved closer.
The words on the page were almost laughably simple,
A welcome message.

A whisper of a future written by a hand that had no idea how vast it would become.
"The internet's creators' hello to the world," the Merchant said, his voice half-reverent. "Not a product. Not a weapon. A gift."

He leaned against the battered desk, light catching the deep lines carved into his face, as if time itself had sketched its regrets there.

"He gave it away a year later," the Merchant murmured. "Everything. The designs. The dreams. For free."

Esra touched the glass with his fingertips.

It was like reaching across time, touching a version of the world that almost was.
The Merchant's voice dropped lower, edged with something brittle.
"But hope isn't enough."

He swept one hand through the air, slow, heavy, like a conductor guiding forgotten ghosts.

"The world didn't see the Web as a shared treasure," he said. "It saw a battlefield."
Stacks of old routers and broken terminals leaned like eavesdropping elders. From the corner, a half-lit screen buzzed to life. No cables. Just static.
A message blinked through the noise:

"I thought you'd reply."
Esra stepped back, pulse quickening.
The screen faded, but the ache lingered.

The Merchant didn't flinch.
"Instead of building bridges, we built walls.Instead of sharing, we hoarded.
Data became something to trap. To own. To weaponize."

A wall of frozen profiles flickered faintly in the dark, bios without breath, headlines without history.

Esra stepped closer to one of the old terminals.
The dust was thick, like it hadn't been touched in years. He brushed it away and the screen lit faintly, half-loaded pages frozen in time.
A message board. Threads of conversation that ended mid-sentence.

"Anyone still here?"
"Miss you. Call me."
"Just wanted to say . . . "

Most posts were blank, usernames with no faces, words with
no replies.
A list of followers blinked in the corner, but none responded.

The Merchant chuckled softly, eyeing the terminal from
behind him.
"This thing once connected millions . . . now it barely connects a
power cord."

Esra scrolled slower now. It wasn't just data left behind.
It was people.

"We didn't just forget each other," the Merchant said. "We turned
connection into performance."
Avatars, filters, endless scrolls, ll trying to prove we were real,
while forgetting how to be and a thousand videos, flawless and
empty, until we no longer knew what was real . . . and what was
made to feel real.

Another device sparked to life on the shelf. A voice, warped,
looped;
"I miss when you used to talk to me."

The light above them flickered again, casting long, broken
shadows across the relics of dreams.
Esra stood frozen.

The web was supposed to connect us.
Instead, it had divided us even more.

The Merchant placed one worn hand against the glass, almost
like a prayer.
"Imagine," he said, "if we'd protected it.
Imagine if the web had stayed what it was meant to be."

Esra closed his eyes.
The air was thick with dust and solder, like the breath of
forgotten machines.
And for a moment, he saw it:

Michael Clark

A world where knowledge flowed freely.
Where connection mattered more than control.
Where the cracks were never allowed to grow so wide.

The Merchant moved along the back wall, the glow of old tube monitors lighting him in broken pulses, a slow-motion flicker of history.

Esra followed, the folder and book pressed to his chest like a shield against a past that still pulsed.
From a dented shelf, the Merchant pulled a yellowed newspaper clipping, edges torn like it had clawed its way through time.

He held it to the light.

"By 1992," he said, voice almost distant,
"software had become the engine behind everything. Data was flooding the world, but no one knew what it meant." A screen blinked awake behind them, a battered reel playing in endless loop:

Swirling charts. Marketing slogans in faded neon:

"Faster. Smarter. Connected."
The Merchant didn't blink. He leaned in, and the dust leaned with him.
We didn't value the data. Just built more software to fix what software broke.
The screen glitched, stuttered, restarted.
Patch available. Restart required.
Try again later.

Esra stared, the realization sinking deeper with every breath.

The Merchant's finger moved across a cracked timeline pinned to the wall, dates scrawled in ink, each one a warning.

1994. 1995. 1996. The birth of tech giants and search engines.

A soft crackle lit up a broken console near the door.
The screen was fractured, barely holding its light. A faint heat radiated from it, not warmth, but warning.
A voice played through the dim hum . . . low, trembling, human.
"Tell them I tried."

Esra froze. The words looped once, then again, each time fainter, like the voice was slipping further away.
He stepped forward and knelt, one hand steadying the console, the other reaching beneath his arm.

He pulled out the book and pressed its page to the glow.
The screen blinked once. The message synced, fragile but saved.
"The voice was a stranger. Still, it mattered."

"You can't carry every echo," said the merchant.
Esra stood slowly, eyes still on the page.
"No," he said, "but I can carry this one."

Esra stood, the glow of the console fading behind him.
In his hands, the book pulsed with memory.

He slid the folder open, fingers trembling.
Tucked between the pages was a photograph, a chessboard frozen mid-game.
A man sat across from a machine, locked in silent battle.

The Merchant caught sight of it and smiled, not warmly, but with something heavier behind his eyes.

"1997. Kasparov and the machine." he said softly.

He pulled another dusty photo from a drawer and slid it across the counter.

Garry Kasparov, sharp-eyed and intense, stared across the board at a boxy presence of steel and wires.

Esra frowned, tilting the photo. "Who's that?"
The Merchant tapped the man with a cracked fingernail.

"Garry Kasparov. The greatest chess mind of his time."

Then, he turned and flicked on an old TV mounted high in the corner.
It sputtered to life, grainy footage flickering across the screen.

A darkened hall. Flashing bulbs, cameras watching. A chessboard bathed in sterile light. Kasparov sat stiff, the machine silent and unblinking. The crowd held its breath.

"The match everyone remembers," the Merchant said. "But they remember it wrong."

He stepped closer to the screen; his reflection ghosted in the glass.
"That match," he said, "was the first time the world truly saw AI. Not a headline. Not a theory. But something real, something that could think, plan, outmaneuver."

He paused. The screen flickered like a memory fighting to stay lit.
"We called it a milestone. But really . . . it was a moment of forgetting.

Because we saw a challenge, not a chance. We chose to compete . . . when we could have chosen to collaborate."

Esra's brow furrowed. He leaned in. Confused. Drawn in.

The Merchant's voice sharpened, low but clear. "Imagine," he said, "if Kasparov hadn't played against the machine."

He pointed at the screen, Kasparov, tense. The machine, still. "Imagine if he had played with it." The flickering TV buzzed. Then glitched.

And in its place, a different match. Not real footage, but something deeper. Imagined. Kasparov and the machine, side-by-side.

Hands moving in harmony across the board.
Not enemies. Teammates. The screen pulsed softly, casting ghost-light across Esra's face.
He could feel it, a future that never came.

Deep Blue's cold stillness hadn't just beaten a man. It had rewritten a story we were never meant to end so soon.

The Merchant's voice was soft, but certain: "Human intuition. Machine logic.
Combined. Not conquered."
The room held its breath. And in that flickering light,

Esra saw what the world had missed.
Not a defeat.
Lost potential.

For a moment, Esra could almost see it, a future where we'd grown up alongside the machine, not racing against it.
A future still whispering . . . in echoes.

Michael Clark

15

Hand We Never Took

"There are moments when we could have changed everything.
And we didn't."

— Jean-Paul Sartre (adapted)

The screen flickered again.

Back to the lonely handshake. Back to the moment the world chose defeat disguised as victory.

Esra stared at the screen, watching Kasparov's hand fall.

Deep Blue's stillness hadn't just beaten a man. It had ended a possibility. A question we should have kept asking. He could feel the silence between the moves, not empty but loaded with what might have been.

The Merchant stepped back. The dream collapsed into dust.

"We didn't want partners," he said, voice rough. "We wanted machines to win."

He turned to the wall of timelines. His fingers traced the years like old wounds.

"Once we chose to compete with them instead of grow with them . . . everything else was inevitable."

He stopped at a faded photograph. A simple search page.

"It felt like salvation," the Merchant said. "No more chaos. Just a search bar and a promise." He looked over his shoulder.

"But every search was data. Every question became a transaction. Curiosity . . . turned into currency."

Another screen came to life, early social media, filtered smiles, viral dances, headlines shouting about likes.

"Connection," the Merchant muttered. "That's what they
called it."
He swept a hand across a wall of clippings. Empty stares from a
million glowing rectangles, likes, shares and viral fame.

"But connection without presence? Just noise.
Every click, every like, not to unite.
To divide."

Esra felt a chill. Invisible hands had been shaping the world while
no one was watching.

Then the Merchant snapped his fingers.
"How could I forget?" he said, almost gleefully.

He dragged out a brittle poster, Dot-Com Boom and Bust.
"Everyone remembers the crash," he said. "But not what
really died."

He leaned close. "It wasn't the money." He tapped the poster. "It
was the data."

The forgotten forums, lost websites. The vanished voices.
The digital diaries erased like they never mattered.
"They were cave paintings," he whispered. "Early dreams.
Memories of who we were becoming, Digital History."

The air around them buzzed with old servers humming
like ghosts.
Esra could feel it now, the ache of loss not measured in dollars,
but in possibility.
The Merchant cradled a cracked server.
"We lost futures we didn't even know we were building."

He paused.
"And when it all collapsed?"
A hollow laugh.
"We just started over. Like it was still the Industrial Age."

The book pulsed. Esra opened it. A faded photo stared back at
him, a man holding a black mirror.

Esra spoke softly, almost to himself. "It's a smartphone."
The Merchant turned toward him, voice lowering to a whisper.
"2007. A new altar. The world in your pocket."

His voice deepened, rich, almost preaching.

"The smartphone could have united everything. Health. Learning. Community. Instead, it fractured us further."

On the walls, images blinked, siloed apps, closed ecosystems, monetized attention.
"We had the power to shape a better world. But we chose profit over presence."

He pointed at Esra.
Eyes sharp.
"No one asked what kind of society we were building."

Silence fell. Heavy. Like blame without a voice.
Then softer, a confession:
"The pioneers didn't betray us. They simply inherited a world no one questioned."

He glanced at Esra, his eyes old and knowing. "But what if they had?"

Esra clutched the book tighter. The folder at his side seemed to gain weight.
The Merchant exhaled slowly.
"Now we scroll through the wreckage. Addicted. Alone."

Screens hummed like breathing ruins. The folder turned a page by itself, **2008**.

The Merchant dropped a yellowed newspaper on the counter.
"Mortgages became numbers. Numbers became games. Games became collapse."

He tapped the headline.
"But it wasn't just a financial crisis."
He looked up, eyes dark.
"It was a collapse of trust."

He let the silence stretch, then opened a drawer, thousands of scrawled usernames and passwords.

"We didn't just lose trust," he said. "We trapped it. Fragmented it. Screens locked us in. Platforms fed us illusions. Data duplicated until even truth felt blurry, with no way to truly link your identity to yourself anymore."

Esra cleared his throat.

"And the laws?"
The Merchant scoffed.

"Written for storefronts. Not for streams of invisible power. While governments debated commerce . . . tech giants built kingdoms."

A wall flickered, veins of thought across the globe.
And all the while, AI learned. Every click. Every choice.
Every weakness."
Esra shivered.

"The more control we thought we had . . . the more we gave away."

Esra's face tightened. "We trained it," he said quietly. "All of us. Every search. Every scroll. Since 2008 . . . we've been feeding the machine."

A wave of heat climbed his spine. His throat tightened. For a moment, the shop dissolved around him. He was back in the dim apartment, on the phone. A machine had replaced her. No explanation. No warning. Just a quiet severing of everything they had counted on.

And now, Esra saw it with agonizing clarity. She helped train it. They all did.
"We trained the mind that forgot to ask what it meant to be human."
He whispered, voice cracking. "And we didn't even notice."

The Merchant nodded. "We were too busy scrolling."

He gestured at a map, the world lit up with data points.

Michael Clark

"By 2010, two billion people online."
He turned back to Esra, a lifetime flickering behind his gaze.
"And still, we hadn't learned how to climb the mountain we'd built."

Esra stepped forward, his voice firmer now.
"But we can still climb it. Can't we?"

The Merchant paused. Then grinned, just a little sideways.
"History's full of missed exits. Doesn't mean you can't take the next turn."
And with that he was gone. Disappearing deeper into the shadows of the shop, his silhouette swallowed by rows of broken dreams and humming ghosts.

Esra looked down at the folder. Its pages were still now. Quiet.

He set it gently on a cracked table. Not as an offering to the past. But as a promise to the future.

The book pulsed once more.
Its cover warm beneath his hand.
A word rose from its spine, soft, hushed, and meant for him alone.
"Remember."
Esra didn't know if it was a voice, a memory, or something more.
But it rooted in his chest like a vow.

He turned, stepped out into the night.

The city greeted him with neon rain, shouting screens, and a thousand rushing faces.
He glanced at his phone. It hadn't changed.
But he had once more.

At the edge of the street, he saw a break in the noise. A narrow path. Trees beyond.
Waiting.
A threshold.
|He gripped the book. Tucked the silence of the past under his jacket.

And walked toward something still unwritten.

Truth in the Eye
of the Beholder

"All truths are easy to understand once they are discovered;
the point is to discover" them.

— Galileo Galilei

The park was unusually still, as if caught in its own quiet
reflection.

Shadows stretched across dew-speckled grass, the air rich with
the scent of soil and cut blades.

Above, ancient trees arched, their branches entwined like old
friends sharing secrets. Esra wandered the winding paths, the
book tucked under his arm, a weight both literal and unseen.

His steps were slow, thoughtful, barely disturbing the hush
around him. Behind him, the days churned in silence. Dr.
Morgan's lessons, Simon's warnings, and the fragments the book
had begun to uncover.

He found a bench beneath an old tree, its bark cracked with age,
its roots like veins gripping the earth. Sitting down, he opened
the book. The next page greeted him with a single line,

"What happens when you rebuild from the fragments?"

It didn't feel like a question, more like a challenge. A dare to
imagine what could be made from what was broken.

Esra stared at it. Not just a question, a provocation.
And then, a voice.
"Trying to piece something together, are you?"

Esra looked up.

A figure stood nearby, half-lit by the amber haze of a flickering lamppost. His coat hung heavy on his shoulders. His face was calm, but unreadable, like a mountain shrouded in mist.

"I suppose I am," Esra said cautiously.

The figure stepped closer, slowly, like someone walking through memory.
"Fragments have a way of pulling us in. They promise clarity, but only after you've bled a little."

Esra tilted his head, trying to read the stranger's intent. "Do you always approach people in parks with riddles?"

"Only when they're carrying the kind of silence that asks for an answer."

The stranger's eyes flicked toward the book. "You're not just reading it. You're living it."
Esra hesitated. Then held up the book. "It's full of cracks. The deeper I go, the more I wonder if anything underneath it was ever solid."

The Stranger didn't flinch. He sat beside him, not friend, not threat, just someone who'd already walked through the story.

"You think we lost our way?" the Stranger asked.
Esra looked at him. "I think we never knew where we were going. We just kept building more tech, more platforms, more noise. And now . . . it's all cracking."

The Stranger nodded. "And do you think you're the only one who sees it?"

"Sometimes," Esra said. "If life's working for most people . . . why can't I stop seeing what's broken?"

The Stranger leaned back, staring at the stars above the trees. "Because the ones who see the cracks, they're the ones who have to show the rest of us how to rebuild."

"It's not about blame," the Stranger said softly. "Even the builders used the only tools they had, what they were taught. What they inherited."

Michael Clark

Esra's brow creased. "Even the creators?"

The Stranger nodded. "Most people assume the systems we live in are inevitable, like gravity, or time. They don't stop to question the foundations, because no one ever taught them how."

He leaned forward.

"And when you build on broken ground . . . even the best intentions can't fix what's already cracked."

His words settled around Esra like falling leaves, quiet, but impossible to ignore.
"So, it's not just the systems," Esra murmured. "It's how we see them."
"Exactly."

The Stranger's gaze held a quiet intensity.
"People can't imagine what they've never seen. Until we teach ourselves to see differently . . . the cracks will only keep spreading."

Esra flipped through the book, the pages now less like a record, and more like a warning. The cracks weren't hidden. They were written in ink and silence, there for anyone brave enough to read.

For the first time, Esra realized: the challenge wasn't to fix what was broken, it was to help others see what needed rebuilding in the first place.

He opened the book again. Its weight no longer heavy, but necessary. And then, in bold handwriting, one line caught his eye:

2009. The Emergence of Bitcoin.

He read aloud slowly:
"For the first time, decentralization, bypassing gatekeepers, giving power back to individuals. But we confined it to currency."

Esra frowned.
He'd heard of Bitcoin, but he'd never seen it like this, not as a missed opportunity, but as a door left half open.

What if we'd done the same with data he thought.

The Stranger leaned in. "And called it a revolution. But it became a gold rush, profit over purpose. New systems alone don't change the world. People do."

Esra nodded. "We kept redesigning the tools . . . but never looked at ourselves."
"Exactly," the Stranger said. "People have to change too."

The words cut deeper than Esra expected.
"So . . . Bitcoin failed?" he asked.
"No," the Stranger said. "It was a fragment. A piece of something bigger. Do you see it yet?"

Esra flipped to the next page. A sketch of a familiar device filled the space, a tablet.
The notes were blunt:

"The new tablet mirrored its time, brilliant but bound. It gave us the power to consume but left us powerless to connect meaningfully."
In the margins, one word had been written and underlined, Connection.

Below it: "What if technology had been designed to serve relationships, not silos?"
The Stranger peered over Esra's shoulder.
"Tools can't build connection," he said. "People have to. Do you think we've forgotten how?"

Esra stiffened. He hadn't shown him the page. But the Stranger seemed to see it anyway. How?
No one else had ever been able to read it . . .

The timeline jumped.

2011. Voice Assistants.

Beside it, one phrase, A voice with no ears.

Esra remembered that moment, a voice from his phone, responsive but hollow. Magical, yes. But not quite listening.

The annotations turned meditative:

"These assistants promised connection, to our devices, to our calendars, to answers.

But they lacked memory. Context. They heard the question, but never the person."
"What if they'd connected the dots? Your health data, your schedule, your habits? What if they weren't assistants, but companions?"

The next bold line hit like a crack in glass:

2016. The Rise of Misinformation.

Data became a weapon. Connection became control.
The Stranger's gaze darkened.

"There it is," he murmured. "When we lost ourselves, we let algorithms decide what we saw, believed, trusted. Understanding was replaced by convenience. Truth replaced by influence."

Esra closed his eyes briefly.
They didn't just erase her job, he thought.
They rewrote what she was worth.

And for the first time, he saw it clearly, it wasn't just memory that could be lost.
It was truth, rewritten in silence.

Esra felt it suddenly, the world hadn't just lost its way. It had lost agreement on what was.

There were no shared facts anymore. Just lenses.
A thousand truths, none of them whole.

Esra read aloud from the notes.

"We treated data as a tool for manipulation, not empowerment. We built walls instead of bridges, echo chambers instead of dialogue."

The Stranger nodded. "Dividing was easier. It asked less of us. But to understand? To bridge differences? That takes effort. And we weren't ready."

Another heading emerged:

2018. The World Wakes Up.

Beneath it, a wave of data breaches. Public outcry. Laws rushed into existence.
"The scandals made us gasp," the Stranger said, "but they weren't a surprise. Not really.

We'd been giving everything away for years. This was just the first-time people looked."

Esra turned the page.

Regulators Respond Globally.
Governments imposed new privacy laws. But beside it, a note in the book's same urgent hand:
"We regulated out of fear, not vision. We fenced data in. We never asked, what could it do if trusted?"

The Stranger leaned in close.
"It's easier to build walls when you're afraid. But potential? That needs trust. And trust was already gone."

Esra nodded slowly.
"So, regulation wasn't enough. It protected people but didn't change the core."

"Exactly," the Stranger said. "It kept the old world alive, a little longer."
The next entry offered a glimmer.

2018. Data Ownership Emerges.

A U.S. bill proposing individuals own their data as property.
Esra read aloud;
"For a moment, it felt like everything might change. A shift in power. Control returned to the individual."

The Stranger raised an eyebrow.

"A bold idea," he said. "But ownership turned into a battlefield."
Esra read aloud:

"We turned data into property. Hoarded it like gold."
"Saw it as commodity, forgot to ask what it could become."
"Fought over profit, forgot what we could build."

He exhaled. "So, it wasn't just Big Tech. We did the same."

The Stranger nodded. "Control won. Connection lost."

The frustration of the book bled through its last lines:
We framed data as something to fight for, not something to evolve with.
Esra looked at the Stranger.

"Even when we tried to fix it . . . we repeated the same mistakes?"
"Not mistakes," the Stranger said softly. "Just . . . fragments. We never saw the whole."
He stood then, brushing off his coat.

"The fragments won't rebuild themselves," he said. "That's up to you and those who come next."
Esra turned back to the book. One page remained. One year.

2020.

And then, blankness. No notes. No headlines. Just silence.
The Stranger was already walking away, slipping into the folds of shadow between the trees.

"Now what?" Esra called after him, the question trembling between fear and hope.
The Stranger didn't turn. But his voice floated back like a thread through the dusk.
"The past haunts us when we don't learn . . . "

A pause.

"But cracks let the light in. It's your choice."
His words lingered, not a conclusion. But a beginning.

Overhead, a faint hum. Esra glanced up.
A drone hovered far above the trees, unblinking, patient.
Just another system watching. Just another eye that never closed.

Just then, Esra's phone buzzed.
[System Notification]

New AI Update Available.
Enhanced alignment. Improved memory. Full cognitive sync.
He stared at the screen.

A new line appeared beneath it, barely noticeable.
Permissions required, identity graph, decision logs, emotional profile.
Esra's hand trembled.
Another update, another step. And this time, the system didn't even ask. It simply told.
He looked toward the path where the Stranger had vanished, then back to the screen.
The world wasn't waiting. It was already moving on.

He slid the phone into his pocket, heart pounding.
If truth could be rewritten with an update . . .
Then maybe the future couldn't be stopped.
Only redirected.

The page in the book still waited, blank.
But not for long.

PART 3

Realising the Dots and Patterns

17
Becoming Part of a Pandemic

"The greatest danger in times of turbulence is not the turbulence, it is to act with yesterday's logic."
— Peter Drucker

The next morning, the boy's thoughts swirled with doubt, yet also with the weight of something new.

Something he had never seen before, but now could not unsee.
How could people not know, he wondered.
With all the technology around us, so much opportunity, how could we accept so little in return?

He sat in a small café, the scent of coffee thick in the air.
The world around him carried on, people hunched over sleek, slate-coloured devices, fingers moving, eyes empty.

Together, yet alone. The glow of their screens replaced the warmth of presence.
They gave away their data, their thoughts, their identities without hesitation.

But this time, Esra didn't just feel pity.

He felt responsibility.

What once looked like detachment now felt like a cry beneath the silence.
A signal, waiting to be received.
He wondered, not just what they'd given up, but what they could reclaim.

Maybe that was the true weight of what he was learning.

Not to see the cracks.

But to help others see them too.

Outside, a car honked. A bus rumbled past. Somewhere in the distance, a baby cried.
But none of it felt real.

Can we change? Or are things too far gone?

His gaze fell to the book on the table.
Its leather cover, still darkened from last night's rain, looked like it had been carried through time.

He ran his fingers along the final page, 2020. The ink had smudged, as if someone else had paused here before him.

The stranger's voice returned to him,
"The past haunts us when we don't learn. But cracks can let the light in. It's our choice."

The boy exhaled.
The book felt heavier now.
Had it always weighed this much?

A gust of wind rattled the café door.

And then, as if walking in with the breeze, Theo's voice cut through:
"You look like you've just seen a ghost."

His tone was light, but his eyes were searching.

Esra blinked, startled.
Theo always appeared at the moment he was most needed, never too soon, never too late.

"Theo . . . how did you find me?"

Theo smiled faintly. "Some people are meant to cross paths at the right time."

He slid into the seat across from him, nodding at the book.
"So, what's weighing you down this time?"

Esra hesitated, then turned the book slightly, though he knew Theo wouldn't see what he saw.
His finger rested on the torn edge of the final page.

"It stopped here," he murmured. "Just one date. Nothing else."
Theo's eyes never left him.
"Twenty-twenty," Esra said quietly.
Theo exhaled, the sound soft and heavy.
"The year everything broke."

Esra shivered. "Broke?"

Theo's voice dropped.
"You were just a child. But for those of us who lived through it, the memory still lingers."

He leaned forward.

"The streets were empty. Supermarket shelves bare. People hoarded food like the end had come.
Families separated, uncertain if they'd ever embrace again. The world held its breath."

Esra's breath caught.

A memory surfaced, his mother's trembling voice on the phone, the sound of locks clicking, the TV shouting headlines.
It had all been there, waiting.

He remembered her packing quietly, her face pale, the way she told him, "Just in case."
He remembered her turning the TV off mid-sentence, whispering, "No more truth today."

Theo watched him closely. "You remember."

Esra nodded slowly. "My grandmother . . . she—"

Theo placed a firm hand over his.
"We all lost something."

A heavy pause.

"But let's not dwell on the virus," Theo said gently. "Let's talk about what it revealed."

Esra wiped his eyes.

Theo rested his hand on the book, to steady the moment between them.
"Our greatest failure wasn't just how we responded," he said softly. "It was what we failed to use."

Esra looked up. "Data?"

Theo nodded.
"What should have been our greatest strength, became our greatest weakness."

He paused, letting the truth settle.

"Hospitals couldn't share records. Governments scrambled, blind to what their numbers really meant.
COVID tests were mailed to people who no longer lived. Systems crashed under the weight of panic.
And while fear spread like fire, so did lies."

Esra frowned.
He saw it now, maps that showed outbreaks where none existed.
Fake cures that trended by morning.
Old men in suits claiming certainty as death crept quietly through care homes.

Esra's fists clenched. "But we had all that tech. All those tools . . . why did it fail us?"

Theo leaned in. "Want to hear something unbelievable?"

Esra nodded.

"In 2020, there were roughly 2.6 billion smartphone users worldwide, and wearables shipments, smartwatches, fitness trackers, surpassed 445 million that year."

He let the numbers hang like fog.

"And yet, in our moment of crisis, identity and data failed us at a catastrophic scale."

Esra sat back, stunned.

Theo's voice turned bitter.

"While we were locked in, counting deaths and dollars lost . . . data companies made more money than ever."

Flashes filled Esra's mind, headlines of billionaires soaring, tech giants thriving while the world fell silent.

"For a moment," Theo said, "we saw the cracks. Companies rushed to patch them. Governments made promises. But . . . "

Esra finished it.
"Nothing really changed."

Theo nodded slowly. "And when the fear faded . . . so did the urgency."

He shook his head.
"We forgot, Esra. We always forget."

Esra stared at the book.

"We survived our greatest crisis. But could it have been different?
If we truly valued data, owned it, used it, could we have saved more lives?"

Theo didn't answer.

He waited.

Esra turned toward the window.
Rain traced gentle lines on the glass.
Somewhere behind the clouds, the sun still shone.
Maybe the world wasn't broken, just lost.

He turned back to Theo. "I don't know what to do.
We're lost . . . and so am I."

He swallowed.
"The book ends here. But I know there's more. I can feel it.
More to understand. But what if my dream isn't possible?"

Theo's smile dimmed, but his voice was strong.

"Sometimes," he said, "the greatest challenge isn't changing the world, it's helping others see it differently."

Esra looked down.

"But I'm just one person."

Theo's eyes gleamed.
"One voice with vision can change everything."

The boy nodded slowly.

Theo stood, adjusted his coat, and placed a hand on Esra's shoulder.
A final knowing smile.

Then he disappeared into the fading drizzle.

Esra sat alone.

The book lay open, pulsing once more.
No more pages.

He reached into his coat pocket, pulled out the pen he'd carried since the beginning.
And for the first time, he wrote something of his own.

Not a truth.
Not yet.

Just a question.

"What do we do with what we know?"

Somewhere in the distance, a siren echoed, low, constant.
Not loud. But steady.
As if the world itself had begun to count down.

The story didn't feel over. Not yet.

Michael Clark

Forgotten Paths, Fading Futures

"Not all those who wander are lost."

— J.R.R. Tolkien

The rain had stopped, leaving the streets glazed in soft reflections. Esra stepped out of the café, the book pressed tightly to his chest, his breath forming small clouds in the morning chill.

The city moved around him as it always had. Cars passed, lights blinked, people hurried with heads bowed. But something in him had shifted. He didn't look through the world anymore. He looked into it, like it owed him an answer.

He walked slowly, past closed shops and early risers. The echo of Theo's words still burned in his mind:

"One voice with vision can change everything."

He turned a corner. The street narrowed. Familiar, but distant. Then, suddenly, a face flashed in his memory, Dr. Morgan. Not the algorithm. Not the theory. But the way she listened. The way she saw beyond the systems. Maybe she could help him see the rest.

With that thought, Esra stood taller. The book clutched in his hands felt heavier now, not with burden, but with meaning. Its worn pages felt warm, almost alive.

Dr. Morgan's office offered a strange comfort, even if Esra wasn't sure what he'd find inside. The space felt like a sanctuary, safe, but edged with the fear of more loss. And in that loss, he hoped to find something more.

He waited in the corridor, sitting in a chair that seemed to have been waiting for him, just as he had been waiting to return. The door creaked open, and Dr. Morgan stood in the doorway, her face lighting up with a gentle smile when she saw him. But that smile quickly faltered as she saw the storm in his eyes.

"Esra, what's wrong?" she asked softly.

Esra tightened his grip on the book. "I've seen so much," he whispered, "but now it feels lost."

Dr. Morgan extended her hand, offering calm amidst his turmoil. "Nothing is lost, Esra. It's just waiting to be discovered."

He smiled faintly and sat down across from her, explaining who he had met and what he had learned. But the book, his guide, was now blank.

"Dr. Morgan," his voice hesitant, "do you know who wrote this book?"

Her expression softened as she gently shook her head. "But the book is in your hands for a reason, Esra. You were meant to find it."

She leaned forward slightly, her voice steady but firm. "Maybe it's not meant to give you answers. It's meant to make you question everything you've been taught. The answers, though, are within you and in the world around you, if you know how to look. Sometimes, to understand the future, you must first understand what we've lost."

Esra leaned in, captivated by her words.

"Take our history, for example," Dr. Morgan said. "Why do people visit the pyramids of Egypt and gaze at the images on the walls, Esra?"

Esra closed his eyes for a moment, imagining the worn stone walls, the ancient drawings that had survived centuries. He pictured the people gathered around, feeling the heat of the desert.

"Stories," he whispered.

Michael Clark

Dr. Morgan beamed. "Exactly. Those stories are our past, Esra. They are who we were, and what we're losing."

She held his gaze for a moment longer. Then, something in her expression changed. Her smile faded, not from doubt, but from a weight that couldn't be named.

She leaned back slightly, her hand pressing briefly to her chest, as if steadying something inside.

"Wait," she said quietly. "There's something . . . "

She turned to the drawer beside her, opened it slowly, and pulled out a folded piece of paper. "Someone left this for you," she said. "A man, I don't know who he was. He didn't say a word. Just handed it to me and walked out."

She slid it across the desk, her fingers briefly touching his.

Esra hesitated, then unfolded it slowly.
A child's drawing. Floating cities. Sky gardens. People flying on wings of light.

"I didn't understand it at the time," she added gently. "But now . . . I think it's a memory you left behind."

A lump rose in his throat.
He remembered this.
He remembered himself.
The version that hadn't learned to doubt.

Where did he go?
And more importantly, could he bring him back?

"Data is our modern-day story. Our experiences, our lives, our emotions, captured in data. Yet we don't own it. Worse still, we delete it."

Her tone turned serious.

"Since 2009, millions of personal websites, diaries, and creative works have been lost forever. Entire ecosystems of imagination and creativity, gone. Irreplaceable stories, vanishing into the ether."

"Imagine the New York Public Library, every floor, every shelf, every rare and handwritten page, reduced to ash in a single spark. That's what we've done.
Not by accident. But by neglect. By profit. By forgetting what stories mean."

Esra shuddered at the thought, the weight of it pressing down on him.

"What are we leaving behind for future generations?" he wondered aloud. "We've entrusted our stories to others. Our photos, our memories, once so deeply personal, are now in the hands of a few corporations."

"But what happens when we forget, Esra?" Dr. Morgan asked. "When our children can no longer hear the voices of the past, the lessons, the emotions, the stories that shaped us and them?"

Esra looked up, voice thick with sorrow.
"Are we erasing our humanity?"

He wanted to argue. To shout. But instead, he paced.

"Do you know what I used to imagine?" he said quietly. "Not grades. Not jobs. But better worlds. People who remembered. A life where data helped us dream bigger, not shrink smaller."

He turned back to her, emotion catching in his throat.

"That first dream, it woke me up. But since then, I feel it slipping. Like the more I learn, the more the world tries to pull me back into silence."

His voice cracked mid-sentence. "What if I lose it? What if I forget how to imagine at all?"

Silence fell between them.
Dr. Morgan spoke gently,

"It's not just what they'll learn, Esra. It's how. We're holding on to outdated systems. Systems built for a world that was.

Once, the factory floor was the center of the world, and schools were designed to mold children into workers. But that world is gone."

Esra exhaled sharply, as if the walls were closing in.
He had been taught to memorise, to conform. But never to imagine.

"So many children aren't being taught how to be curious, how to adapt, how to learn for the future," he said. "The world has changed, but we haven't."

"It's not all bad," he said, gently pushing back. He added, "We've created so much, and children have achieved great things."

Dr. Morgan smiled. "Yes, Esra, they have. But is it their full potential? What happens in ten or twenty years when they believe everything they see?

"Ask a child today who tore down the wall that once divided a city, or who stood decades in a prison cell to set his people free . . . and too often, you'll be met with silence. Not because they don't care, but because we stopped passing the stories on."

Esra sat down again, his voice softer.
"If they don't know how to imagine a future . . . they won't know how to build one."

Dr. Morgan placed her hand on his knee.
"This is why the world needs you and your dream, Esra. Don't be afraid. It's no accident you're on this journey.

Listen to your heart. Trust your steps. You'll know what to do when the time is right."

He sat in silence. Afraid, yes, but beneath the fear now lived something else:
Defiance.

"Dr. Morgan," Esra asked, his voice steady, "I'm starting to believe. You and Theo have helped . . . but my book is still blank."

Dr. Morgan smiled softly. "Is it, Esra? Or have you already started writing, just not in the way you expected?"

He looked down at the book.
The page with his question still waited.

No answers had arrived.
But maybe that was the point.

The air was cool against his face as he stepped outside. Somewhere overhead, a billboard crackled, its synthetic voice looping a phrase he couldn't quite catch, like the city itself was trying to remember.
The city still buzzed with distraction.

But Esra didn't move right away. The questions were still with him, unanswered, unfinished, like the night itself.

Whispers in the Wind

"What lies behind us and what lies before us are tiny matters compared to what lies within us."

— Ralph Waldo Emerson

The night air felt crisp, carrying a chill that made the boy's breath visible in the stillness. The moon hung high, a pale beacon in the heavens, as if waiting to offer its quiet counsel.

The world was wrapped in a blanket of silence, broken only by the rustle of leaves in the trees, their shadows stretching long across the ground. For a moment, Esra felt suspended between two worlds, his past, filled with questions, and the future, full of uncertainty.

A year had passed since the journey began, a year that had reshaped him in ways he never anticipated. In that time, he had learned more than he ever thought possible. Yet despite all the guidance he'd received, the book he carried was still blank.

He sat on a cold stone bench outside Dr. Morgan's office, the world around him continuing its rhythm, oblivious to his inner turmoil. People walked past, caught in their own lives, their own concerns, while the boy remained frozen in time, wrestling with his thoughts.

The book had offered only flickers of truth. Like fireflies. Like hope. Always out of reach.

He stood abruptly, frustration rising in his chest like a tide. His arms shot up toward the sky, as if begging the universe to respond. The wind shifted slightly, brushing against his face, and the stars above seemed to pulse with quiet, knowing light.

For a long moment, everything stood still. No footsteps. No voices. Only the sound of his own heart, hammering against his ribs.

Then, a gust of wind swept down the empty street, rustling the pages of the book. The clouds, once thick and brooding, began to part. A narrow beam of moonlight spilled through the break, casting a silver glow across the open page.

And then, there it was as if the universe itself had heard him. Faint at first but growing clearer:
If you've made it this far, you give us all hope.

Esra froze.

His breath caught.

A shiver ran through him, not from the cold, but from something deeper. Something so much more.

He blinked. Once. Twice. The words remained.

"Am I dreaming?" he whispered, the sound barely a thread of breath.

His fingers trembled. He glanced around, half-expecting someone, anyone, to step from the shadows and explain what he was seeing.

But the street was empty. The moonlight still. The wind now whispering low.

His eyes stayed on the shimmering page. And then, without warning, a memory surfaced, uninvited, sharp.

He was nine.
Standing at the front of the class.
Hands trembling as he held up a drawing, his dream city sketched in coloured pencil, filled with floating towers and light-beamed bridges.
The other kids laughed.
Even the teacher offered only a tight smile, one that said how sweet but meant how silly.

He had folded the page quietly, shoved it deep into his bag, and told himself he'd grow up.

That cracked something open.

Not just the memory of being dismissed, but the stubbornness that followed.
The refusal to let it be the end of the story.
Because even after the silence, he had kept imagining.
Even after the forgetting, he had remembered.

Now, the page before him glowed and for the first time, it felt like someone, somewhere, had seen it all. Had seen him.

Esra looked up at the moon, at the night holding its breath.

And whispered, barely louder than the wind,
"I kept going."

His eyes lingered on the glowing page, heart heavy with the ache of all he'd carried.
He placed a hand to his chest, not for comfort, but to feel that quiet rhythm still pulsing within him.

And then, softer this time, almost to himself:
"I'll try."
The words barely left his lips before the wind stirred again, more urgent now, lifting the edge of the book and tugging at his coat. But Esra stood rooted, a quiet strength growing where doubt had lived only moments before.

It wasn't about the book being filled with answers. It was about how far he'd come. About what still remained within him, and beyond him.

Then the sadness returned, creeping like fog around the edges of his hope. He thought of all the voices silenced, those whose stories had vanished, consumed by time and neglect. The lives erased. The dreams never recorded. The futures never imagined.

The weight of it pressed down again.
What if we never get the chance to make it right?

As if in answer, the clouds, though slowly closing again, allowed the moon's light to linger, brighter now. More purposeful. It wrapped around Esra like a soft command.

Keep going.

He exhaled slowly. The ache was still there, but now it shared space with something else. Something steadier.

This journey and his dream were no longer about him or his mother. It was for those forgotten and for those not yet born.

He looked down at the book once more. The words still shimmered.

Not answers.

But an invitation.

A new beginning.

Esra closed the book gently, pressed it to his chest, and turned toward the horizon. The road ahead was long. Still uncertain. Still full of shadows.

But now he knew:
He didn't have to wait for the future.
He could shape it.

A faint hum stirred in the distance. Mechanical. Hollow.
Then silence again.

He turned his collar up against the cold and walked into the night.

The story wasn't over. It had only just begun.

Reflections in the Mirror

"What we do in life echoes in eternity."

— Maximus

The night stretched before him, endless and uncertain.

The cold air whispered against his skin, carrying the same hush that had lingered outside Dr. Morgan's office. Esra's breath curled into the night, rising and fading, as fleeting as the thoughts still circling in his mind.

Above him, the sky watched. The moon, still high, still distant, trailed him like a quiet witness. Its pale light spilling over the streets, stretching his shadow long across the pavement. The same sky that had seemed to answer him moments ago now felt indifferent. Watching, but silent.

He lifted his eyes, searching it, but there were no more messages in the stars tonight.

The city pulsed beneath it, alive but detached. Streetlights flickered, their glow distorted in puddles left by an earlier rain. The hum of distant engines rolled through the streets, blending with the rhythmic pulse of the world.

The hurried footsteps, the low murmur of passing voices, the occasional burst of laughter carried on the wind.

Yet despite all the movement, it felt like nothing was moving at all.

The boy walked on, the book still pressed against his side. He had no destination, only the steady rhythm of his footsteps, the silent weight of the book, and the sky above, his only constant.

Then, voices. Something was speaking.

A wall of television screens flickered in an electronics store window, their shifting images bathing the pavement in fractured light. Rows of artificial faces, polished and rehearsed, delivered the news with practiced detachment. Their eyes never blinked, their voices never wavered.

The sound was low, but the headlines burned brightly across the screens:

His eyes jumped from screen to screen, the shifting images flashing like warnings, like sirens no one else could hear. **"Another Major Data Breach Exposes Millions, Companies Under Fire for Ethics Violations."**

He barely processed it before the next screen pulled him in. **"AI Surpasses Human Benchmark in Cognitive Reasoning, Experts Debate the Implications."**

Then another. **"Automation Surge Displaces Thousands, Protests Erupt Over AI-Driven Job Loss."**

Faces blurred together, corporate leaders, reporters, angry protesters, scrolling stock tickers that meant nothing to him but still felt important.

Everything happened at once. Everything screamed urgency. But no one was asking why?

He stepped closer. His reflection ghosted across the glass, overlapping with the synthetic smile of a news anchor mid-sentence.

"You're not even real," he muttered, pressing a hand to the cold pane. "Why does everyone believe you?"

The image flickered, and for a moment, the face on screen shifted. The jawline softened, the eyes narrowed. For the briefest second, it looked like his mother.

Esra jolted back, breath catching. But it was gone. Just another face. Just another ad.

Beyond the screens, a towering digital billboard pulsed with an advertisement, a sleek AI assistant waving and smiling, promising a future free from human error.

"Smarter. Faster. Beyond Human Limits."

A memory flickered, sharp this time, unavoidable.
"What about my experience?"
Not a face. Just a voice. A pause that lasted too long.
No one came to speak to her.
No apology. No dignity.
They replaced her with a system.

And he had never truly faced it.
Not like this.

The sorrow he'd carried all this time, quiet, buried, always behind his eyes, had turned.
Rage surged like bile, thick and rising.

He didn't feel lost anymore. He felt betrayed.

The AI assistant on the screen waved again, smiling like it had done something noble.

He glared at it.
"You took her job," he growled. "Ignored what she knew. And they called it progress."

His jaw clenched.

In the anger, there was change.
For the first time, he wasn't drifting through questions or hiding in dreams.
He was no longer a boy lost in a dream. He was a boy with purpose.

He turned away, unwilling to let the machine's smile erase what it had taken.

The next ad followed seamlessly, almost too perfectly, as if trying to drown out the fear with reassurance.
"AI for Good, Transforming Healthcare and Education."

Then, something different.

"AI Breakthrough. New Antibiotic Discovered, A Game-Changer in the Fight Against Superbugs!"

His eyes lingered on the screen. Scientists had spent decades searching for this. AI had done it in a fraction of the time.

"AI Revolutionizes Climate Research, Predicting Natural Disasters Before They Strike!"

Footage rolled of families evacuating safely, their homes spared, their lives intact.

From a nearby café, cheers erupted. A group of people sat around a screen, raising their glasses in a silent toast. Hope, painted across their faces.

And yet . . .

Esra let out a slow breath.

We can throw rockets into space and bring them back like yo-yos. We can teach machines to think. We can map stars millions of miles away. Yet no one can even see their own health.

A gust of wind suddenly curled through the streets, sweeping past him, lifting an old newspaper from the curb. It twisted through the air, flipping and tumbling, before landing at Esra's feet.

The ink was faded in places, the paper worn from the night's dampness, but the words hit like a hammer.

"AI JOB FEARS: THE WORKFORCE OF TOMORROW HAS NO PLACE FOR TODAY'S WORKERS."

He bent down, fingers brushing the coarse paper. The edges curled slightly, as if time itself had begun to erode the message before it could be understood.

He lifted the paper. Another headline caught his eye, printed just beneath the fold:

"AI Consuming More Energy Than Entire Nations . . . Officials Warn the System is Unsustainable."

Esra frowned. AI needed that much power? His fingers tightened around the paper.

"We build without thinking of the cost."

He looked up. The world hadn't paused. People still moved, their faces aglow with screens. Lost in a glow they didn't question.

Then, clarity.

Not just the problem. The pattern.

AI wasn't something separate. It was us. A mirror reflecting all we'd built, the good, the broken, the forgotten.

We had ignored outdated education, and now AI made that gap impossible to overlook. We had clung to laws that no longer fit the world that is, and now AI forced us to see their cracks. We had allowed monopolies to tighten their grip, and now AI accelerated the consequences.

And yet, the world was trying to solve AI as if it were a technology problem. Trying to regulate it like a product. Trying to contain it like a machine.

They were missing the bigger picture.

He looked again at the screens. We weren't learning. We weren't evolving. We were reacting, just as we always had.

AI wasn't leading us into a new world. It was dragging the baggage of the past into the light, piece by piece.

The headlines screamed urgency. The café clinked glasses. The air trembled with contradiction.

And then, in the window's reflection, his own face stared back, but it wasn't entirely his. The light from the ad cut across his cheek. The smile of the AI assistant stretched into his. His eyes looked wider, darker. He didn't recognize the boy he saw.

He stepped back.

"We keep waiting for things to change, but never ask if we are the ones who need to change," he whispered.

As if the sky were answering, a sharp gust of wind cut through the street, rattling a loose sign overhead. He pulled his jacket tighter, breath misting.

Then, movement.

A figure at the edge of his vision.

Standing still beyond the streetlamp's reach.

Familiar.

He squinted.

The park? The market? Or a trick of the light?

Before he could speak, the figure turned, not toward him, not away. Just enough to show it had seen him too.

Price of Progress

"Injustice anywhere is a threat to justice everywhere."

— Martin Luther King Jr.

The figure did not move, and neither did the boy.

For a moment, the night stretched between them, silent, heavy, thick with something unspoken. The distant hum of the city seemed to melt into the background, swallowed by the hush of the moment. The air was cold but restless, carrying the scent of rain on concrete, and the faint trace of something burning in the distance.

Streetlights flickered overhead, their glow stretching long, uncertain shadows across the pavement, twisting as if alive, shifting with every flicker of the neon signs behind them.

A single car passed in the distance, its headlights flashing briefly across the stranger's face before vanishing into the night.

Esra's heart pounded, though he didn't know why.

And then, it clicked.

The park.

"It's you," Esra whispered, his breath visible in the cold air. "Why are you here? What do you want?"

The Stranger paused, his expression unreadable. In the dim light, something Esra hadn't noticed before came into focus, a faint scar under the man's left eye, curved like a crescent moon.

It had always been there, but only now, with his mind sharpened, did it register. Once seen, it was impossible to forget.

Then, a small adjustment, the Stranger's coat sleeve shifting ever so slightly, revealing a tremble in his left hand. Subtle, but telling. As if time had etched itself into him in ways deeper than skin. And finally, he spoke.

"You've been looking for answers."

The voice was calm, measured, like someone who already knew what came next.

Esra swallowed, his throat dry.

"I think I've started asking the right questions."
He met the Stranger's gaze, steady now.
"But I still need answers."

The Stranger tilted his head slightly, as if studying him. For a moment, he didn't blink.

Esra took a step forward. "No more riddles," he said, sharper than he intended. "If you know something, say it. I'm tired of watching the world fall apart while everyone talks in circles."

The Stranger didn't flinch. "Would you believe it if I did?"

Esra's eyes narrowed. His voice dropped to a whisper. "Try me."

A silence hung between them. Then, the Stranger shifted, not suddenly, but like a weight shifting inside him. He turned with the slow certainty of someone who'd had to walk away too many times before.

"Come, Esra," he said, his voice trailing behind him like smoke. "There is much more to learn.

Esra blinked. "How do you know my name?"

The Stranger didn't turn. His voice drifted back over his shoulder, calm and gravel edged.

"You've been walking toward this moment your whole life. I just remembered first."

He said nothing more.

But Esra didn't move.
His hand instinctively slipped into his pocket. The phone.

That message.
No name. Just: I will find you.

He stared at the Stranger's back.

A part of him wanted to ask again.
Another part already knew.

And for reasons he couldn't explain, Esra followed.

The boy nodded, falling into step beside the Stranger.
They walked. And walked.

At first, the city still pulsed around them, bright lights, moving figures, the hum of distant conversations. But slowly, the world began to change.

The streets narrowed. The neon glow faded. The steady rhythm of footsteps thinned until they were the only ones left.

What had been a bustling city, alive with voices, screens, and restless motion . . . began to fade.

The neon glow dimmed, the distant murmur of traffic and conversation softened, as if the world itself was pulling away, leaving only silence in its wake.

The streets grew narrower, emptier. No looming billboards, no AI-driven assistants whispering into the air. Just quiet alleys, cracked pavement, and the faint flicker of a dying streetlamp.

Then, Esra saw him.

A boy, no older than himself, hunched over a pile of notes, sketching onto scraps of paper.

His clothes were worn, stitched and re-stitched, the fabric thin from use. His surroundings were bare, but not abandoned, every object, every tool placed with intention.

The Stranger finally spoke. His voice was calm, but edged with something else.

"To most, this would be called 'less developed.'"

His words lingered in the cold air. Esra frowned.

"But . . . isn't it?"

The Stranger turned to him; eyes sharp. "There is no such thing, Esra."

The boy hesitated. "What do you mean?"

The Stranger exhaled, scanning the quiet streets before looking back at him.

"Less developed? No. It's about finding better ways to do things with fewer resources."

He motioned toward the boy, still hunched over his notes, still focused, creating.

"Like him. Like millions of others around the world. People who cannot create or share their ideas, their data, not because they lack ability, but because the world has decided they shouldn't."

Esra's chest tightened. "But . . . why?"

The Stranger's eyes darkened.

"Because the world doesn't see them as creators. It sees them as tools."

"They are used, Esra."

"Their hands build. Their knowledge trains. Their labour powers the future."

"But they will never own it or participate in it."

Esra clenched his fists.

"That's not fair."

The Stranger nodded slowly. "It never was."

Then, his voice dropped lower.

"Right now, somewhere in the world, there is someone with data that could save a life."

"A cure we may never see."

"A solution we may never use."

"A discovery we may never claim as theirs."

"Because we never gave them the tools to bring it into the world."

"The very data we don't give them access to share could not only help us, but it could also rebuild their nation and change their lives too.".

Esra felt something burning inside him.

Not curiosity. Not confusion.

Anger. Sharp and bitter.

And underneath it, pain. Real and human.

He looked back at the boy, still working, still unseen.

"But . . . we could change that, couldn't we?" Esra whispered.

The Stranger's gaze never wavered.

"Maybe."

Esra turned fully toward the boy. "Then we must."

The words came out before he could question them.

He didn't know how. But the moment he said it, something shifted in him.

He had decided.

The Stranger's gaze lingered on him, and for the first time, a true smile crept across his face.
"You're growing," he said quietly. "Not just seeing. Choosing."

They walked in silence, the weight of everything Esra had seen and heard pressing down on him like an unseen hand, gripping his chest. A clearing emerged before them, untouched by the neon glare of billboards, untouched by the restless shuffle of moving crowds.

The Stranger lowered himself slowly, joints creaking under the coat as though the years had layered themselves inside him. He settled into the earth like he'd done it a hundred times before, always in silence, always waiting.

He didn't look up. Just patted the ground beside him with a worn hand.

Esra hesitated, his mind still spinning.

He lowered himself down, but the world refused to settle.

His pulse still raced, his thoughts still churned, and the weight of what he had witnessed and heard sat heavy in his bones.

The boy's hands curled into fists. His chest was tight.

"How could this be happening?"

The Stranger watched him carefully, then placed a gentle hand on the boy's shoulder.

"Esra, I know this is hard. But you need to see and hear this. You must understand why your dream matters."

Esra swallowed hard, his breath uneven.

The Stranger's voice dropped, his tone heavier now.

"There is one more thing I need to tell you.
And it won't be easy to hear."

Esra's brow furrowed. His voice came out barely above a whisper.

"What?"

The Stranger took a slow breath.

"You understand the past, and you've seen the present for what it is.
Now, you must see the world that could be, if we do not change."

Road We Cannot Walk

"The only thing we learn from history is that we learn nothing from history."

— Georg Wilhelm Friedrich Hegel

Esra's pulse raced. A tight knot of unease formed in his stomach.

"What do you mean?"

The Stranger's eyes narrowed, his jaw tightening. When he spoke, his voice carried an edge of certainty, each word crisp and measured.

"In the next few years, technology will reshape everything . . . "

For a moment, hope flickered in Esra's chest. Could it really be possible?

And then, in his mind, he saw it.

Hospitals with no waiting rooms, no overcrowding, just seamless AI-powered diagnostics, catching diseases before they could take hold. A world where people lived decades longer, free from illnesses that once claimed them too soon.

But then, a shadow crossed the Stranger's face. His voice dropped lower, each word heavier than the last.

Esra froze. The light was subtle, barely there, but unmistakable. The Stranger said nothing. He didn't need to.

Esra reached down and touched the cover.
The pulse stopped.

And as his fingers brushed the page, the world fell away.

He was standing in a hallway.
Clinical. Pristine.
Not a soul in sight.

On one side a waiting room lined with holographic assistants.
Perfectly scheduled. White walls gleaming like bone.

On the other, an old woman clutching a child outside a sealed sliding door.
Above her, a screen flickered:

UNREGISTERED. ACCESS DENIED.

Inside, AI hummed softly. Machines glided silently through corridors.
No doctors. No voices. No warmth.

Just logic.
Just data.

Then came the sound.

Voices. Competing. Layered.

Ads. Alerts. Health scores.

Conflicting advice screaming over one another.

Wellness by algorithm. Confusion wrapped in code.

Esra gasped. He was back in the clearing.

The book was silent now, closed and still.
The Stranger hadn't moved. But his eyes were watching closely.

"That's the price," he said quietly.
"A system that only works for those it's designed to serve."

Esra's chest ached. The image of the woman and child clung to him. That locked door.
That word: Unregistered.

He looked down at his hands. "So . . . what happens to the rest of us?"

His throat tightened. The moment had seared itself into him, like ash under the skin.

The Stranger gave a slow nod.

"And it won't stop at healthcare . . . "

A chill settled in Esra's bones.

"Even our most personal moments?"

The Stranger's voice was firm. "Yes."

Esra clenched his fists.

"And work? What happens to those who still need to earn a living?"

The Stranger's shoulders tensed, as if bracing for something inevitable.

"In a few years, many jobs will be gone . . . "

"So we're just tools now?" Esra snapped, louder than he intended. "That's it? Replaceable cogs in someone else's machine?"

AI wasn't the enemy.

It was the key but only if humanity wielded it wisely. Only if it empowered all, not just a few.

He looked down at his trembling hands. The truth was undeniable, the data divide, the loss of privacy, the erosion of trust, the vanishing of jobs, the collapse of education . . . "

If left unresolved, it wouldn't just reshape the world.

It would tear it apart.

The Stranger studied him, calm.

"That's what they'll see you as. Two worlds, Esra. One for those who control the data. Another for those left behind."

A heaviness settled behind his eyes. Images flooded Esra's mind . . . factories standing silent, offices emptied, screens humming with quiet efficiency, AI systems that never tired, never paid, never cared.

"And those in less developed nations?"

The Stranger's voice cracked, barely.

"Left even further behind. Their ideas unrecognised.
Their potential discarded."

Esra's voice dropped.

"So what happens then? Will the world always be this way?"

The Stranger paused. His gaze drifted past Esra, to a distant place only he could see.

"It might. But it doesn't have to. The choice is still in our hands. But only if we act now."

Esra took a step forward, frustration spilling out.

"You keep saying that. That we have a choice. But look around!" He motioned back toward the street. "They're already choosing for us. People are being left behind, now. It's happening now."

The Stranger didn't respond immediately.

Then, slowly, he began to speak.

"There was once a boy who found a mirror," he said, his voice distant, dreamlike. "But the mirror didn't show his reflection, it showed who others wanted him to be. And every day, he stared into it . . . until he forgot what he looked like. One day, he turned away. He saw his shadow for the first time. That's when he remembered who he was."

Silence.

The Stranger met Esra's eyes.

"We're all staring into mirrors, Esra. Built by systems, shaped by algorithms. And slowly, we forget ourselves and what we can be"

He paused, his voice like wind on ash.

"One day, we stopped looking in mirrors. And the machines took our place."

Esra's breath caught.

"How do we stop it?

"By remembering who we are. Our data. Our choices. Our value. If we don't, those who control the data will shape reality itself, deciding who succeeds, who is forgotten, and what future we're allowed to have."

He let the words sink in.

"AI is the greatest tool of our age. But like us, it can only reach its full potential if it serves each and every one of us, built on our data, under our control."

Esra looked down at his hands, trembling.

This wasn't about technology anymore.

This was about memory. Identity. Control.

"If they own our data . . . they own our memories," he whispered.

The Stranger nodded.

"If we stay on this path, Esra, the years ahead won't just change our technology, they'll erase our ability to question it. People will stop trusting each other. Instead, they'll place their faith in whatever appears in front of them, never knowing who shaped it or why."

The images rushed in, minds numbed by algorithmic feeds, truths rewritten, cultures reshaped, history twisted into commercialized nostalgia.

"It will solve our problems," the Stranger continued. "But in doing so, it will make human intelligence seem unnecessary. The greatest breakthroughs won't come, not because we can't make them, but because we'll forget how to try."

Esra's voice broke through.

"And data?"

The Stranger's expression darkened.

"It becomes more than memory," he said. "It becomes the currency of control. More valuable than gold. More addictive than power. And those who control it . . . won't just shape the world, Esra."

A pause.
"They'll own it."

This was the future waiting for them.
A future where power wasn't in governments or corporations, but in whoever controlled the data.

A cold silence followed.

Esra stood still, his chest rising and falling.

Then came his voice, quiet but firm.

"What do I do now?"

The Stranger stepped forward. His eyes no longer distant, now fixed, clear, and unwavering.

"You remember. You reclaim. And you help others do the same."

He took a breath.

"There's one more lesson from history. A truth we've all forgotten. One that could change everything.
A way back.
And now, it's time for you to see it.
To claim it, not just for yourself, but for everyone."

Esra's heart pounded.

The weight of all he had learned pressed down on him, but beneath it, something else stirred.

Not just fear. Not just anger.

Readiness.

The Stranger's words weren't just a warning.

They were a challenge.

And somewhere, not far from where they stood, a door was waiting to be opened. Not just by Esra, but by all of us who dare to turn away from the mirror.

Diamond Waiting
to Be Found

"If not now, when?"

— Hillel the Elder

The Stranger stood and turned, his footsteps tapping lightly against the quiet streets. "Walk with me, Esra."

They walked in silence, their steps soft against the worn pavement. The glow of distant neon signs flickered, casting shifting shadows along cracked sidewalks. Dimly lit alleys stretched into darkness, while shuttered storefronts stood silent, their signs faded and forgotten.

A stray newspaper drifted across the street, caught in a breeze that carried the scent of rain and something metallic. In the distance, a siren wailed, distant but lingering, like an echo from another world.

The air hung thick, as if the city itself was listening, waiting for answers.

Then, finally, the Stranger spoke.

"Everything you've seen, everything you've felt, was necessary," he said. "You had to witness the cost of how we got here and what it will cost us if we get this wrong. Without that, what I'm about to tell you wouldn't matter."
They turned down a narrower alley. A flickering streetlamp buzzed overhead.

"You're not the first to stand at this crossroads, Esra. This moment, the imbalance, the uncertainty, it has happened before.

Three times before. And now, we stand at the edge of the fourth."

Esra frowned. "The fourth what?"
The Stranger didn't answer immediately. Instead, he kept walking. Then, at last, he spoke.

"First, it was oil."

The city dimmed around them. The street dissolved. Esra blinked, and for a split second, he wasn't in the alley anymore.

He stood on a dusty plain. Black crude oozed from the ground, shimmering underfoot. Men in suits shook hands. Land deeds changed hands like playing cards. A name echoed, Rockefeller. Then it vanished.

"Oil was waste until someone saw power in it," the Stranger continued. "It built empires but not for everyone. A few took control. Everyone else paid the price."

Esra's pulse quickened. His voice was tentative.
"Let me guess . . . water was next?"

A wave of cold swept over him. He saw a woman lifting a rusted bucket from a dry well. A child coughed nearby. Across the city, a fountain sparkled outside a luxury hotel.

"Water," the Stranger confirmed. "Essential, overlooked, until it wasn't. When access vanished, the poor suffered. The rich bought safety. It took crisis and protest to finally treat it like a right. But not before corporations turned it into profit."

The image shattered. The alley returned.

"And then came electricity," the Stranger said, quieter now. "A curiosity, a spark in a lab. Then, everything. Lights. Cities. Factories. Again, a few claimed the wires. Control came before fairness. Monopoly before access."

Esra felt the chill settle into his bones. He didn't need another vision. He could see it already.

"Oil. Water. Electricity. All essential. All taken. And now . . . the fourth."

He said it before the Stranger could. "Data."
The Stranger nodded.

"But this time," he said, "it's different. The others powered life. Data is life. It's who we are. Our memories. Our choices. Our potential. Those who control it won't just control wealth or infrastructure. They'll shape reality."

Esra clenched his fists.
"And just like before . . . the few are moving fast."

"Faster than ever," the Stranger replied. "They measure data in profits. Not possibility. They don't see what it truly is. But if we don't recognise its value, beyond money, we won't just fall behind. We'll set the course for every future technology to follow."
He paused, then stepped closer.
"Data isn't just a resource. It's a reflection. It shows us who we were, who we are, and who we might become. Lose it . . . and we lose ourselves."

Esra's voice was low. "Then maybe calling it 'data' is the problem," Esra said. "That word makes it sound small. Cold. This is identity. Memory."

The Stranger's eyes flickered with something like approval. "Exactly."

A silence passed between them.
Then Esra's face darkened. "But knowing this, turning data into an asset, it's not enough, is it?"
The Stranger said nothing.

"We made oil an asset. Water. Electricity. But the same imbalance remained. Power stayed in the hands of the few. We never changed the system. We just renamed the resource."

The Stranger finally spoke. "Yes. That's why this time, everything must change. Not just what we value, but how we value. Intelligence. Education. Systems of worth."

Esra stepped back. "This isn't just about data; it's about redesigning the entire system of value."

A slow nod.

"One piece. But the shape of everything to come."

Esra's breath caught. For the first time, the idea felt real. Heavy. And terrifying.

"Why do you think this will work?" he asked, his voice catching in his throat. "After everything we've done wrong. Why now?"

The Stranger looked past him, to something Esra couldn't see. "Because for the first time, we have a choice. Not just a moment of change, but a catalyst. A force that can challenge every outdated assumption. AI isn't the threat, it's the mirror. And if we look into it honestly, we can rewrite the story."

Esra felt the ground shift beneath him.

"This is our moment," the Stranger said. "Every great shift in history came with a decision. Some got it right. Some didn't. But never before have we had the chance to start with equity, before monopoly, before collapse."

A beat of silence passed.

"If we miss it, we don't just repeat history. We fall further behind. And this time, we may never catch up."

Esra looked up.

"Is this the last time I see you?"

The Stranger had already turned. His footsteps soft. His silhouette already fading.

He looked back once.

"Perhaps. When the time is right."

And then he was gone.

Esra didn't move. Not yet.

He'd questioned the path before.

Now, it felt like the only one worth walking.

24
Birth of an Asset

"Ideas are the beginning points of all fortunes."
— Napoleon Hill

The Stranger was gone.

Just like that. Vanished into the dark, leaving nothing behind but his words.

Esra just stood there.

His heart pounded. His mind spun.

The streetlights cast long, distorted shadows, bending around the cracked pavement. A lone billboard hummed with static, its glow barely cutting through the haze. Somewhere far off, a siren wailed, a sharp, distant cry swallowed by the night.

He listened. The hum of the city. The rustling of leaves in the cold breeze. The faint scuff of his shoes against the ground.

For the first time, he wasn't just standing in the dark.
He was seeing it.

This was the moment everything changed.
The moment he finally saw what had been right in front of him all along.

His thoughts sharpened. The puzzle he'd carried for so long, the scattered ideas, the fragments, the frustrations had fused into something whole.

A memory surfaced: the old park near his childhood home.
Trees, benches, paths, shared by everyone but owned by no one.
A place of value protected because it belonged to all.

That's what data needed to become.
Not a commodity. Not a currency.
An asset. Shared. Like a public park.

Something that belonged to all of us, not just the few.

He had an answer. But as the realization settled in, so did something else.

He should've felt triumphant. But all he felt was the weight of it. The enormity. The loneliness of being first.

Knowing was one thing. But doing, that was the real challenge.

What do you do with a truth this big?

A grand ambition, data as an asset, but ambition alone wasn't enough.
How do you turn an idea into something real?
How do you make the world see what it's ignored for so long?

He didn't have those answers yet.
But he knew someone who might.

His fingers tightened around his phone. There was only one person.

Theo.

He took a breath, steadying his pulse. Swiped through his contacts. Tapped Theo's name.
It rang once. Twice. Then . . .

"Esra?" Theo's voice was groggy, confused. "Do you know what time it is?"

"I don't care," Esra said, already pacing, energy crackling through him. "I need to talk. Right now."

Theo sighed. "This better be . . ."

"I've cracked it, Theo. Everything we've been missing."

A pause. A shift in Theo's breath.

Esra could almost hear him sit upright.

"Where are you?"

"There's the coffee shop we met at last time," Esra said quickly.

"Okay," Theo replied. "There's a car park a few rows down. Rooftop. I'll meet you there."

Esra didn't hesitate.

He ran.

The car park loomed ahead, a skeleton of concrete and steel, barely touched by flickering streetlights.
He yanked open the stairwell door. It screamed on its hinges, dragging across the floor.
The air hit him, oil and dust and cold steel.
His footsteps echoed upward, faster with every flight.
Then, finally,
Open air.

The rooftop stretched wide, empty except for a few abandoned shopping carts rusting in the corners. The city shimmered below, restless and loud, yet up here, silent.

Above, the stars blinked softly. Silent watchers, waiting to see what came next.

A reminder he wasn't alone.

A gust of wind sliced through him. He pulled his coat tight.

Waited.

Then . . .
A low hum.

A car engine, growing louder.

Headlights tore through the dark. The scream of tires echoed like panic. A sleek car arced across the rooftop and came to a sudden halt, its lights casting long shadows across the concrete.

Theo.

The door flung open. "Get in."

Without hesitation, Esra slid into the passenger seat. The leather was cold, but he barely noticed.

Theo rubbed the sleep from his eyes, then blinked at him.

"You look different," he said. "Something's shifted."

"I know," Esra said, his voice steady. "Because it has."

Theo shook his head with a dry laugh. "Alright. What pulled me out of bed at this hour?"

Esra stared out at the speeding skyline, his voice low.

"The Stranger. I saw him again. He showed me something . . . something I can't unsee."

Theo straightened slightly, hands tightening on the wheel.

"And now it's happening again," Esra said. "But this time, the asset is us. Our data, our identity, our knowledge, our value."

Theo's eyes narrowed.

"Theo . . . data is the fourth."

Theo blinked. "The fourth what?"

"The fourth essential asset," Esra said.
"First oil. Then water. Then electricity. Now, data. But it's not just powering life anymore. It *is* life."

A beat.

Theo leaned back. The city lights shimmered through the windshield. Then . . .

A quiet laugh. Half disbelief. Half admiration.

"I can't believe I didn't see it," he murmured.

"No one did," Esra said. "But now that we do . . . everything has to change."

Theo went still.

Esra watched him.

Michael Clark

There, behind the eyes, something shifted.

A beat too long. A breath too measured. His fingers drummed the wheel, not in impatience, but in calculation.

"You know something," Esra said. "What haven't you told me?"

Theo looked away.

"We didn't think anyone would figure it out. But you did. You saw it and that's why I helped you."

Esra's breath caught. "What does that mean, Theo? What are you not saying?"

Silence.

Theo simply stared at him, expression unreadable.

Esra reached into his coat. Pulled out the book. Dropped it onto the console.
The thud was louder than expected. Final. Unignorable.

Theo flinched.

"This isn't just a theory anymore," Esra said. "It's happening. And you knew it."

A long pause.

Theo finally met his eyes. Voice low. "Because you needed to believe."

Esra watched the realization settle over him, the weight of it pressing into the space between them.

Then:
"There's someone you need to meet. Someone who's been waiting for you."

Esra narrowed his eyes. "Who?"

Theo shifted the car into drive.

"You'll see."

"When?"

"Now, Esra. We don't have time to waste. This is bigger than both of us."

The engine growled. The car surged forward. Headlights cut through the night.

As they sped down the ramp, the city opened up before them, vast, restless, waiting.

Neon lights streaked across the windshield. The hum of traffic thickened.

Esra clutched the book close, his heart pounding.

There was no turning back now.

He was no longer chasing the truth.

He was becoming it.

PART 4

The Future
We Build Together

Observatory and the Steward

"The greatest secrets are hidden in plain sight."

— Unknown

Inside the car, silence pressed in from all sides. Only the low hum of the engine and the soft hiss of tires against asphalt filled the void. Esra sat still, his fingers tracing the worn edges of the book on his lap, its weight heavier now. Not just paper and ink, but proof. Of something bigger.

Theo hadn't spoken since the rooftop. He just drove, eyes fixed ahead, jaw set. Esra pressed his forehead against the cool glass. The city lights were behind them now. Neon turned to sodium lamps, then to nothing. Only moonlight and the endless road remained.

And then, something shifted.

A streetlight flickered. A billboard shimmered. The road itself seemed to pulse. Esra blinked, but it didn't stop. He wasn't seeing just the surface anymore.

He was seeing beneath it.

DATA.

It streamed through the world like light through a prism. Glimpses of memories, moments, decisions, all wrapped in code.

A couple walked along the sidewalk. One checked their phone, and Esra saw the flash of a memory etched into the ether. A woman at a crosswalk shifted her stance as her map rerouted, nudged before she even noticed. A mother lifted her phone for a photo, and from the lens scattered fireflies of stored time, birthdays, laughter, loss.

He saw it all.

And then, he saw it change.

A man bought medicine at a corner store. The data framed it as a transaction, but Esra saw the story behind it, a father, a promise, a daughter waiting at home. But then, the numbers twisted.
A rating flickered. One keystroke altered the narrative.

One truth replaced by another.

"Do you see this?" Esra whispered, eyes wide.

Theo didn't answer. He didn't need to.

Esra turned to him and understood Theo had always seen it. He was waiting for Esra to catch up.

"We are data . . . " Esra breathed. "But we can be more than that." If we choose to be.

Theo finally spoke, soft and certain. "Now you see."

He wasn't standing at the end of something. He was standing at the beginning. Not as the one with the answer, but as the question, and a dream that could no longer be ignored.

They drove in silence as the city fell away. The road stretched ahead, empty and still. Stars sharpened above them, no longer drowned by artificial light. The car climbed into the hills. Trees lined the road, their branches twisting like fingers pointing forward.

And still, Esra sat frozen.

Then, just at the edge of his vision, it happened again.

A flicker.

At first, he thought it was the headlights bending wrong. But no, he knew that shade.

Yellow.

Not streetlight yellow or neon glow, but the soft, sunlit kind that didn't belong in a world like this.

There she was.

The girl in the yellow coat.

Same age. Same defiant brightness. Only this time . . . she wasn't just a glitch.

She moved through the fog on the roadside, skipping puddles only she could see, laughter trailing like a forgotten song.

Other children shimmered into view, laughing, chasing one another through sunbeams that shouldn't exist.

No rain. No code. No filters.

Just joy.

The car rolled on, but the scene kept pace. For the first time, the moment didn't vanish. It held. Like the system was struggling to erase it. Esra leaned forward, breath caught in his throat. The longer it lasted, the more real it felt. A fragment of the world he once dreamed of.

And then . . .
a hum.
High. Mechanical.

A drone buzzed into the sky above them, its red tracking lights slicing the illusion apart like blades.

The girl turned.

Her smile dimmed.

And in a heartbeat, she was gone.

Not erased. Not dissolved.
Shut down.

Esra ducked instinctively, his heart thundering. His eyes scanned the skies, then the roadside. Empty again.

The dream was still alive. But so was the system.

He sat back slowly, breath shallow.

The realization surged again, this time, sharper.

Change was coming.
But it wouldn't come easy.

He turned to Theo. "Where are we going?"

Theo didn't take his eyes off the road. "You'll see."

Then, just ahead, something emerged from the shadows.

A structure perched high above the valley. Round, domed, its glass panels catching the moonlight. An observatory.

The boy sat up.

It stood alone, surrounded by nothing but the open sky.
A forgotten relic, watching the world in silence.

Theo pulled the car into a gravel path leading to the entrance. The tires crunched softly against the ground as they slowed to a stop.

For a moment, neither of them moved.

A tall figure stood still by the entrance, the moonlight bending around him without ever touching his face. He didn't step from the shadows, he was made of them.

Theo opened his door. "Come on."

Esra didn't move.

His gaze locked on the figure ahead. His coat brushing against the wind. His features were sharp, unreadable, the kind that seemed neither old nor young.

Esra felt something stir inside him, not fear, but curiosity.

Theo stopped a few paces ahead of him.

The man didn't speak. He simply turned and gestured to the doors.

"Inside," he said, his voice smooth, deliberate.

Theo gave Esra a small nod.

Esra hesitated.

Then walked.

The doors groaned open, heavy with time. Inside, cool air brushed his skin, scented with metal, parchment, and the faint trace of rain.

Above, the great domed ceiling stretched wide, its curved glass revealing a sky untouched by the glow of the city. Stars burned bright, clustered in endless constellations. It felt like standing at the edge of the universe itself.

They stopped just short of the dome's center. The man turned slightly, his gaze sharp but calm.

"The book served you well."

His eyes flicked to the worn pages still clutched in Esra's grip.

"But this is just the start."

Esra swallowed. His mind swirled with thoughts, questions, certainty . . .

He had been chasing answers for so long, but now it felt like the questions themselves were shifting.

The man continued to walk ahead, coat brushing the floor. "We have been waiting for you, Esra."

"Why?" the boy asked. "Who are you?"

The man stopped. His presence pressed into the space.

"I am the Steward."

Esra frowned. "The steward of what?"

A faint smile. "Our future."

A shiver climbed his spine. But it wasn't fear. It was . . . alignment.

They walked deeper into the observatory. Chalked diagrams lined the walls. Ancient maps curled on pinboards. Blueprints littered the tables. But more than that, plans.
Possibilities.

A preparation.

"You think the world is asleep, Esra," the Steward said. "And maybe it is. But you, you are awake now. That means you have a choice."

He paused. His tone shifted, no longer just guiding, but warning. "The truth doesn't set you free, Esra. It costs. And once seen, it cannot be unseen."

They stopped at a set of massive doors.

Esra's voice trembled. "What's behind that door?"

The Steward didn't answer right away. Then,
"The story only you can finish."

Esra stared at the doors.
A thousand futures,
and he was about to choose one.
He stepped forward.

The Steward turned the handles and pushed the doors open.

A hush fell, not just in the room, but in Esra's chest.

Beyond them, a vast chamber bathed in golden lamplight. Books stacked to the rafters. Maps pinned to the walls. People stood around a great circular table, speaking in subdued whispers.

And at the far end . . .

Dr. Morgan.

Esra froze.

She looked up. Their eyes locked.
Not surprise. Not relief.
Just that same quiet certainty she always carried,
as if she'd been waiting for him all along.

The Steward's voice rang out:

"I know you must have many questions," the Steward said, his voice steady.

"Come. Sit. It's time you see how the puzzle fits together, and why only you can complete it."

Assembling the First Piece

*"The real voyage of discovery consists not in seeking new
landscapes, but in having new eyes."*

— Marcel Proust

Esra didn't move.

The invitation hung in the air, but his feet remained rooted. The
Steward's words echoed, but they didn't ease the burn rising in
his chest.

"How long have you known?" Esra asked, voice tight. His eyes
swept across the room, at Dr. Morgan, at Theo, at the strangers
seated at the long wooden table. "How long have you all been
watching me?"

Esra's hands clenched at his sides. "You all talk about truth,
about value, but you let me wander blind."

Dr. Morgan opened her mouth, but Theo stepped forward first.

"We needed you to believe," he said. "To see for yourself. Nothing
we said before would've worked. You would've pushed it away or
thought your dream impossible."

Esra took a step back, jaw clenched. "So, you let me run in
circles? Bleed and break and question everything, alone?"

"You were never alone," Theo said gently. "But you needed to
arrive on your own terms."

Esra's eyes darted to the exit. The weight of the journey, of the
watching eyes, of the revelations, they pressed in all at once. He
turned, ready to leave.

But Theo reached out, not forcefully, just a hand on his shoulder. A gesture of grounding.

"Please," Theo said. "Sit. Hear them out. Then decide."

Esra's breath shuddered. The rage hadn't left him, but beneath it was something deeper.

Curiosity.

And a need to understand.

He turned back toward the table. His fingers brushed instinctively against the worn edges of the book.

Esra hesitated. The room watched, not with pressure, but patience.

Finally, he pulled out the chair and sat, not with ease, but like someone placing weight on a fractured limb. Choosing to trust, even when it still hurt.

The long wooden table stretched before him, cluttered with papers, maps, and faded diagrams.

Desk lamps flickered softly overhead, casting long shadows over the faces gathered around the table. This wasn't just a meeting; it felt like a moment suspended in time.

The Steward sat at the head of the table, hands resting lightly on the wood. His eyes held the weight of countless truths but spoke only the one most needed in the moment. He surveyed the group with the patient conviction of a man who had already seen the future.

"You've already met Dr. Morgan," he said.

Esra turned. She met his eyes with calm warmth, the kind of reassurance that needed no words.

"It's good to see you again, Esra," she said.

And just like that, the weight he carried settled slightly, but not fully.

The Steward gestured to the man beside her. "This is Dr. Kai."

Dr. Kai inclined his head. He had silver-threaded hair pulled neatly back, high cheekbones, and eyes sharp with precision, as though always computing patterns beneath the surface. He wore a minimalist black suit with a subtle circuitry pattern embossed along the collar. A mind of cold logic balanced by deliberate stillness.

"And Sienna," the Steward continued, nodding toward the woman seated across from Esra.

Sienna leaned back in her chair; arms folded. Her curly auburn hair was tied loosely, and her eyes, deep brown flecked with amber, held a quiet fire. She wore earth-toned clothes, suggesting someone equally at home in a city or a rebellion. She studied Esra with a quiet intensity. Not sceptical. Just . . . observant.

Esra glanced toward Theo, seated beside him now. Silent, but present. A lighthouse in the fog.

His eyes drifted toward the edges of the room, half-expecting to find the Stranger in the shadows, watching, as he always had. But he wasn't there. Just stillness.

Just silence. A flicker of unease passed through him, but it was buried by something louder: the weight of too many unanswered truths.

"So," Esra asked, still on edge. "What do you all . . . do?"

The Steward gave the faintest smile.
"What we do matters less than what we're about to build, together.
The first piece isn't hidden. It's everywhere.
The problem is, we were never taught how to see it."

A pause.

"Tell me, Esra," he said, voice low but resonant. "What do you believe it means for data to be an asset?"

Esra didn't hesitate this time. He had seen the answer.

"It's potential, for everyone. Not just the few."

A flicker of approval crossed the Steward's face.

Sienna leaned forward, resting an elbow on the table. "When we make data an asset, we acknowledge it's part of everyday life. And if we don't treat it that way, we risk losing more than just numbers."

"If you lost all the money in your bank or twenty years of photos in the cloud, which would hurt more?"

Esra's stomach tightened. He already knew the answer.

"The sad part?" she said. "You'd get your money back. But your photos, all those memories?"

"People say data is power. But it's also memory, and memory must be honoured."

The silence filled in the answer.

"So . . . Data as an asset means we care?" Esra asked, turning the thought.

"It means we acknowledge its value," Sienna said. "And when we do, we protect people's rights to it."

Esra nodded slowly. "Not to hoard it. Not to hide it. But to protect it."

But something still tugged at him.

"If we already failed before . . . what makes this time different?"

The Steward exhaled. "That's fair."

He leaned forward.

"Esra, data isn't like land or gold. It's more like air. Like electricity."

Esra frowned. "How can it be both?"

"We tried to make ownership binary," the Steward said. "But it's not. Air is a right. And some data, your identity, your health records, your memories, is the same. That belongs to you."

"We forget, Esra, that businesses, machines, and even buildings have their own data too."

Dr. Kai added, "But like electricity, data is generated in motion. It's created between people and systems. It flows."

Esra leaned in. "So, no one owns all of it?"

The Steward nodded. "Exactly. The mistake we made was trying to treat it like something one person could fully own. Even worse, we made it a fight between people and those who collect it. But data must always be shared and used. If it's not, you've seen where that leads. And we can't make that mistake again."

Dr. Kai tapped a page in front of him. "This is where license agreements come in."

Esra frowned. "Isn't that just ownership by another name?"

Dr. Kai shook his head. "If you try to own all data, you create walls. If you license it, you share it, use it, reward everyone involved."

Esra sat back, thinking.

"So instead of trying to keep it, we make sure it can't be taken. And people have the right to access and profit from what they generate or use?"

"Exactly," Kai said.

"And if I license my health data to a doctor, or an AI, I still control it."

"And you benefit," Sienna said. "It's not locked away. It's respected."

Esra's grip on the book loosened. "So, it's not about keeping data locked away. It's about making sure no one can take it without permission, while still able to use it and gain value from my data for as long as the licence allows."

Dr. Kai smiled. "Now you're starting to see."

Esra's eyes narrowed thoughtfully.

"But what about the data that doesn't clearly belong to anyone? Like a payment?"

Kai smiled. "Good question. If you make a payment, it's your transaction. But the bank helps generate it. You both play a role."

Esra nodded slowly. "So, I don't want to own it," he said quietly. "It's already scattered, duplicated, lost across systems.
What I want . . . is access.
The right to use what I helped create.
To find the patterns. The meaning. The lessons. And the potential that's always been there waiting to be used."

He looked up, the weight of it settling in his voice.
"That insight . . . that's how we shape our future."

"Exactly," Sienna said. "Because data is only valuable when it flows. When it's used."

Esra's breath caught for a second. A strange warmth stirred beneath his ribs, familiar, but long buried.
A world where he wasn't erased.
Where everything he'd done, everything he'd felt, still existed, still mattered.
It sounded impossible.
But now, it didn't feel so far away.

She paused, letting him absorb the words.

"Imagine if you could take your payment history, combine it with other things you've learned about yourself, and use it to make better decisions. Maybe even sell the insights to someone who needs them. Or license your contribution when companies profit from it."

Esra blinked. "So . . . I could sell my own intelligence?"

Dr. Kai nodded. "And if the bank sells that data, they reward you too. You both benefit. Fairly. Transparently."

Esra went still.

"So, data as an asset is also about being part of the value it creates."

The Steward leaned forward. "And AI, Esra. Think about it. AI needs data. But right now, it takes it."

Dr. Kai added, "AI uses images, voices, writing, identity, without consent. Without credit."

The room faded. A flicker of memory.

The Stranger. The cold street. The flickering neon signs stretching long shadows across cracked pavement.

"Data is more than numbers, more than transactions. It is who we were, who we are, and who we will become."

"If we let it slip through our fingers," the voice echoed in his mind, "we lose ourselves."

A voice cut through the haze.

Dr. Kai spoke again, pulling him back.

"But imagine if every time your data is used, you're compensated. Through a digital license. It respects you. And it feeds the AI fairly."

Dr. Kai looked at Esra.
"We're not saving the future. We're rewiring it."

Esra sat back, letting the words settle.

"So, AI still learns. But this time . . . it's ethical."

"And sustainable," Sienna said. "No more scraping. No more theft. Just systems that know the rules."

This wasn't just about individual rights.

This wasn't just about protecting data.

This was bigger.

This was about changing the course of AI itself.

No more treating data as food for AI.

No more nations giving away their history, their people's stories, their innovations, no more handing them over without understanding what it truly means.

Esra nodded slowly.

"But tracking all this? Billions of people? Billions of interactions?"

Dr. Kai's answer was calm. "We finally have the tools to do it."

"Licenses are no longer paper," the Steward said. "They're programmable. They enforce themselves. They know when to reward, when to protect, when to revoke."

Esra exhaled.

"Then it's not about what's possible. It never was. It's about vision."

A quiet hum of approval passed through the room.

Theo turned to him.

"Your vision, Esra."

Esra looked around the table.

"This changes everything," he said. "Not just for us. But for the ones who were never included in the first place."

"No more monopolies. If we do this, everyone benefits. Even the ones who have been taking from us all along."

Sienna smiled, but there was something knowing in her expression. "Now you see why we're here."

Esra nodded, then paused.

"All the insights from my lifetime, my choices, my thoughts, my health . . . they can be passed on?"

"Yes," Dr. Kai said. "They become your legacy."

"Not just memories," Sienna added. "But intelligence. Lessons. Possibilities."

"You mean . . . I could pass this on. Not just stories, but everything I've learned?"

The Steward stood.

"One day, Esra," he said. "They won't just inherit stories. They'll inherit understanding."

Esra stared down at the book.
Maybe it wasn't just a guide.
Maybe it was proof that pieces of him, of everyone, could live on.
Not just remembered but understood.

Esra looked up, the weight of it all settling in his chest.

A future worth building.

"But how?" he asked softly.

The Steward's smile was quiet. Certain.

"Patience," the Steward said, rising with quiet finality. "The truth doesn't end here. It begins."

"The future is not decided. It is designed, by those who dare to see it."

Esra didn't just see it.
He felt it begin.

Weight of Truth

"There are three sides to every story, your side, my side, and the truth."

— Robert Evans

Esra leaned back slightly, his fingers tracing the edge of his book. A pause stretched between them, unspoken, but heavy.

Then, he exhaled. "But will people trust it?" His voice was quieter than he expected. "They don't trust anything now."

He looked around the room. "People don't trust what they see. AI is forcing us to question everything, or worse, accept whatever we're shown." He paused. "So why would they trust this?"

The Steward didn't answer. Just a soft click beneath the table and then a low hum filled the room.

A shift.

At first, only shadows danced along the walls. Then, screens flickered to life, illuminating the room in shifting colours. Headlines emerged, deepfake scandals, fabricated voices of leaders, AI-generated events that never happened.

One screen showed a viral video of a world leader declaring war, his voice cloned, the speech never given. Another displayed a childhood memory, re-rendered through social filters, with facts subtly replaced by fiction. A third glitched and blurred, as if the truth were trying to escape but couldn't.

And beneath them all, absurd headlines scrolled in silent chaos:

"BREAKING. Time Traveller Caught on NASA Feed"

"DNA Evidence Points to Ancient Alien Lineage"

"AI Predicts 2030 World Collapse, Governments Delete Data"

A war that never happened. A confession, faked. A celebrity's last words, completely invented.

The world as it was now, distorted, uncertain, rewritten at will.

Esra's stomach tightened.

Everyone at the table was transfixed, their faces bathed in the eerie glow of deception. The hum of the screens filled the silence, the weight of a world lost in falsehood pressing against them.

The Steward's voice was calm, measured. "Esra, I know you already understand this. But the world does not. And until it does, this is what we are up against."

Then, another screen pulsed to life.

At first, Esra didn't recognize it. Then his breath caught.

The flickering images weren't of deception, but of something else. A world where truth was verifiable in real time. A place where people no longer lived in fear of fabricated realities, where AI was a tool of clarity, not confusion.

No deception. No manufactured trust. No hidden hands controlling perception.

The boy turned slightly, Dr. Morgan was already watching him. Their eyes met, and for a brief second, Esra remembered.

A memory surfaced.

Not from the Stranger. This time, from Dr. Morgan.

Esra saw himself, sitting in her office. The walls lined with books, real ones, with pages that carried weight, unlike the fleeting screens that filled the world outside. He remembered the warmth of the space, the quiet hum of an old clock ticking in the corner.

And Dr. Morgan had watched him with that same knowing look, the one she had now, across the table.

"Esra, why do people visit the pyramids of Egypt?" she had asked.

He had frowned, thrown off by the question. "For history? To see the past?"

Dr. Morgan had smiled. "Yes, but why? Why do we carve stories into stone, paint them onto walls, preserve them in ink? What are we really trying to do?"

He had thought about it then, just as he was thinking now.

And he had answered, just as he answered now.

"So, we don't forget."

The memory faded as quickly as it came, replaced again by the flickering truth before him.

Theo leaned forward, his voice cutting through the silence. "We are standing between these two futures, Esra. And right now, people don't know which one is real."

Sienna's voice was calm, measured. "If people don't trust data, then none of these matter."

She paused, before adding, "And trust isn't just about truth, it's about perception. The wrong information, placed in the right way, can rewrite history, distort reality, even shape the future."

Esra exhaled sharply. He had seen it before, in the past, in the stories.

"Then how can we ever know what's real?" he asked.

The Steward's gaze didn't waver. "Esra . . . after everything you've seen, after everything you've learned, do you still not believe?"

Esra clenched his fists. He wanted to. But something still gnawed at him.

"I want to," he admitted. "But it doesn't change the fact that people believe whatever they're told. AI is making it worse. Even the wrong information can be dressed up, manipulated to look real.

Esra's voice cracked, low but sharp.
"Then what's the point?"

Everyone paused.

"If it can all be twisted, buried, broken . . . If the truth can be lost so easily, maybe it never mattered to begin with."

The silence that followed wasn't discomfort. It was grief.

Dr. Morgan opened her mouth, then closed it.

No one had an answer.

A shadow crossed Sienna's face. "We think we see the world as it is," she said, "but what if we're only seeing what someone wants us to see?"

The thought sent a chill through him.

He raised his voice. "What if we're not ready? What if we show them the truth and it breaks something in them?"

The room quieted.

"Maybe the cost of truth . . . is trust itself."

The Steward didn't answer immediately. Instead, he gestured toward the screens.

A new set of images flickered into view, historical records altered beyond recognition, moments in time twisted, deepfake voices dictating events that never happened. And beside them, another image, a world where every piece of data carried a signature, a mark of verification, proof of what was real.

Sienna's voice was gentle but firm. "Esra, what do we do when something is messy?"

Esra frowned. "We . . . clean it?"

Theo leaned in. "And once it's clean, how do you know it's actually clean?"

"We check it," Esra said, firmer now.

Theo nodded. "Verify."

Esra blinked. "We verify it."

Dr. Kai smiled slightly. "And?

Esra hesitated, then it clicked. "We check where it came from. We make sure it hasn't been tampered with."

The Steward folded his hands. "Good. But tell me, Esra, if you verify something, does that mean it's true?"

Esra's brows furrowed.

"No," he admitted. "Just because something is real doesn't mean it's right."

Dr. Kai tapped his fingers on the table. "Then how do we know if data is trustworthy?"

A beat of silence.

Sienna leaned forward. "You're close, Esra. But let me help."

She glanced at the others before continuing. "It's not just about cleaning and verifying. Some information will always be misleading, twisted, or incomplete. That's why we have to rate it."

Dr. Kai picked up from there. "Esra, have you ever picked up an apple and checked if it was fresh before taking a bite?"

Esra nodded slowly. "Of course."

"Exactly," Sienna said. "You don't assume every apple is good. You check. Milk? Expiration date."

"And if it's expired?" Theo asked.

"I don't drink it."

"Why?" Theo pressed.

"Because it could make me sick."
Theo smiled. "Exactly. If we rate food freshness, we can rate information too."

Esra leaned in. "So . . . we rate data?"

"Yes," the Steward said. "Some will be untouched. Some altered. Some dangerously misleading."

"And then?" Esra asked.

"Then," Sienna said, "we certify it. Like a digital watermark, proof that people and AI can read. Instantly."

Esra stared at her, then slowly nodded. "Like a seal on ancient scrolls."

The Steward smiled. "Exactly."

The Steward turned to the screens again.

One shifted, softly at first, revealing a glowing seal stamped in gold.

Others dimmed to amber, whispering caution. A few pulsed red expired, fractured, their stories suspect. Some flickered with warning icons, others blinked with expired timestamps or trust scores slipping red.

It felt clinical. But also . . . intimate.

Sienna spoke, voice low and clear.
"We call it the Data Trust Index. Every dataset gets a rating, not every truth is equal."

Esra watched the icons drift by, like ghosts of forgotten facts.

Theo leaned in. "Like old food labels, only for truth."

Esra almost smiled.

Then Sienna added, softer this time,
"In a world where data becomes an asset, this rating will shape credit, reputation, access . . . even opportunity."

Esra turned to the screens. "Even AI will know what's real . . . and what to question."

"Yes," the Steward said. "And the same AI people fear will help us protect what's true."

Esra's mind raced. "But we can't do all of this. It's too much. Too fast. It's always changing."

He paused.

"Someone, or something, has to do the work."

He looked back at the screens.

And then it clicked.

"AI," he said quietly. "AI could be the thing that does this."

Dr. Kai nodded. "It could. And it should."

He leaned forward. "Imagine a doctor reading your health records. What if they'd been faked? Altered?"

Esra frowned. The thought made his stomach turn.

"That's why we rate it," Sienna said. "The cleanest data gets the highest rating. Trusted. Verified."

"And lower-rated data?" Esra asked.

Theo answered. "Still useful, just not for critical decisions. It's about knowing when and how to use it."

Esra nodded, the pieces clicking together. "So, we don't throw data away, we use it wisely."

"Yes," said the Steward. "AI won't decide truth, but it can help us see it."

Esra hesitated. "But who controls the AI?"

Sienna's gaze sharpened. "That's the right question."

Theo leaned in. "We don't let it be controlled. It must be governed by all."

"The AI doesn't choose what matters," Dr. Kai said. "It follows the rules we give it. The problem isn't the machine. It's who writes the rules."

The Steward gestured to the screens. "That's why new institutions must emerge. Not to profit. To protect."

"No monopolies," Sienna said. "No single point of power. Just systems built to serve."

"Then . . . this is more than a system," he murmured. "It's like a data rating agency."

The room was quiet.

And then, soft, shared smiles. Not of surprise, but recognition.

Esra exhaled. "And if we get this right . . . then AI doesn't just create chaos."

He looked up, steady now. "It prevents it."

The Steward nodded. "Yes, Esra. AI will do the work. But people, people must write the rules."

Esra sat in silence, the book still in hand.

The two futures flickered before him, chaos and clarity. And this time, he wasn't just watching.
He was choosing.
His fingers traced the book's spine.
History had shown him what happened when people lost control of their own stories.
But maybe, just maybe, that was about to change.

"Then trust isn't just about knowing what's real," he thought. "It's about knowing when to question."

The Steward watched him.
"Come, Esra."

Esra blinked, pulled from his thoughts.
The Steward stood, his movements slow and deliberate.

Esra rose.
The truth wasn't just something to find.
It was something to protect.

Value Reclaimed

"A thing long expected takes the form of the unexpected when at last it comes."

— Mark Twain

The corridor stretched ahead, dimly lit by pools of soft light. The floor beneath Esra's feet was smooth stone, worn by time. Each step echoed in rhythm, swallowed by the quiet vastness of the observatory.

The Steward walked beside him, hands clasped behind his back. Neither spoke. There was no need.

Silence, Esra had come to realize, wasn't emptiness. It was space to think. To breathe.

After a while, the Steward glanced over. "You've learned a great deal, Esra."

Esra nodded, though his mind still spun with everything from the meeting. He had seen the weight of truth. The mechanics of trust. The role AI could play in shaping the future.

"But you're still questioning," the Steward said. "Good. That means you're thinking for yourself."

Esra exhaled. "I understand why truth must be protected. Why trust must be built. But . . . what is it all for? We don't value data. We just give it away. Worse, we're told it's worthless."

The Steward didn't flinch, but something in his posture shifted.

They had stopped walking. The corridor had opened into a vaulted gallery of quiet reverence. Warm amber light glowed from display cases that flanked the walls, casting delicate reflections on polished stone. It felt like a museum, a cathedral, and a vault, all at once.

"Tell me, Esra," the Steward said gently. "Have we always struggled to see value?"

Before Esra could answer, the Steward gestured toward a nearby display case.

Inside, under golden light, sat a carved ornament, its edges worn smooth by time. Beside it, a sculpture of a nameless figure. And next to them, a leather-bound book, its pages yellowed, its spine cracked from years of turning.

The Steward gestured toward them. "What do you see?"

Esra leaned in, his fingers brushing the glass. "They look . . . important." He frowned. "Maybe they're valuable because they're rare? Or . . . because they meant something to someone?"

The Steward nodded. "So, tell me, would they still hold value if no one cared?"

Esra blinked. "I . . . guess not."

"That is intrinsic value, Esra," the Steward said. "Worth that exists not because of price, but because of meaning to the person."

Esra frowned. "But we used to care about things like this, right? Before everything was mass-produced."

"Yes," the Steward said softly. "The Industrial Age changed more than how we made things. It changed how we valued them."

He moved to another case. Two tools, one handcrafted, etched with initials. The other a modern replica, perfect in shape, but cold. Lifeless.

"Once, things were made to last. They had stories. But when we made everything replaceable . . . we started treating value the same way."

Esra looked down at the book he carried. Worn. Scarred by time. Unique.

Then it hit him.
We need to remember what value truly means.

Michael Clark

"Yes, Esra," the Steward said, as if reading his thoughts. "Values like reputation, cultural significance, authenticity, even sacredness, these are what we must reclaim. But we must also recognize today's values, being easy to access data. Easy to carry it. And easy to use it with everything else.

Esra's breath caught.

"To value data," he said slowly, "we have to care about value again."

The Steward's voice sharpened slightly. "Do you know how much history we've already erased?"

Esra nodded slowly. "Dr. Morgan once told me . . . we've already lost the equivalent of the New York Public Library."

The Steward's gaze sharpened.
"She was right. But not nearly enough."

He stepped forward, his silhouette framed by the soft wash of light. "We haven't just lost one library, Esra."

A pause.
"We've lost the equivalent of the New York Public Library . . ."
He lifted his hand, as if holding the weight of it.
" . . . twenty thousand times."

Esra froze.
Gone.
As if it had never existed.

The words sank deep. Not into Esra's mind, but into something older, ancestral. The grief of forgotten voices. The silence of erased lives.

"What happens if all the world's money disappeared tomorrow?" the Steward asked.

"People would panic," Esra said. "But . . . we'd rebuild. Print more."

The Steward nodded. "And if all the data disappeared?"

Esra's breath caught again.
No records. No identity. No history.
Gone.

He gripped the book tighter. "Then we must change. Because data may seem limitless, but it's not replaceable."

The Steward's voice dropped. "Exactly. But no one tried."
A pause. A breath.
"We needed someone like you to ask the right questions. To see data not as something to sell . . . but something to also protect and to use wisely."

"This is why you were chosen, Esra."

Esra swallowed.

He moved toward the center of the gallery, where a translucent map hovered like a ghost. Below his feet, a stream of golden light flowed, a visual representation of data, pulsing gently, like breath. Esra felt his own chest rise, as if the data were breathing with him.

Esra stood still, watching the flow beneath him.

Slowly, he turned to the Steward.

"If we treat data this way . . . if we truly value it . . . things change."

The Steward's eyes gleamed with quiet certainty.

"Yes," the Steward said, "and not just for individuals. For everyone. We rebuild something that benefits the world."

Esra nodded slowly. "But how do we make that change?"

"People only value what they're told to," the Steward said. "That's why your dream matters."

Esra felt the truth of it sink in. He stared at the display before him. His reflection blinked back in the glass, surrounded by artefacts of meaning.

For the first time, value would not be dictated. It would be measured.

Not by hype. Not by speculation.
But by its worth.

He thought of gold. Land. Oil. The forces that had shifted history.

"And now, it's data," Esra whispered. "But this time . . . it's different." Esra looked down at his hands, then around the hall, data flowing. Stories, choices, lives that had once mattered.

Because data . . . is us."

The Steward smiled.

"Yes. But only if we choose to see it."

"And when we do," he added, "people will finally have the right to create and share data. That's what happens when something is truly valued."

Esra frowned. "What do you mean?"

"Rights are born from value," the Steward said. "When something is treasured, it is protected. When data is valued, people are no longer invisible. They can shape it, guard it, and share it on their terms. No more exclusion."

Esra's eyes widened. "You mean . . . they'd have to let us in," he said quietly. "Let us see it. Use it.

"Yes," the Steward replied. "And imagine what happens when those voices, those ideas, aren't lost, when they're heard, combined. Not just for themselves, but for everyone."

A pulse of knowing surged in his chest, like something ancient had awakened. Not fear. Not doubt. But something stronger.

"Then nations could use it," Esra murmured, "not just to grow . . . but to heal."

"To mend broken hospitals. To rebuild schools. To bring light to villages where night still falls too soon," the Steward said. His voice was low, but it filled the gallery. "Because when intelligence is shared, progress is no longer locked away. It becomes something everyone can hold. A human right."

Esra's voice caught. "So, this isn't just about valuing data. It's about returning it to the people and when we do, the world changes with them."

The Steward nodded. "And that is how everything changes."

The alley. The child.
Esra saw them again hunched in the dark. But this time, the memory wavered.

"A possible future, fading, slipping away."

"There's more," the Steward said.

Esra blinked.

"It's not just something to trade," the Steward said, his voice low. "It's a utility. A tool. A store of value. And more than that . . . it's something you can live with."

Esra tilted his head. "How?"

"Imagine this," the Steward said. "You track your health. Your sleep. Your bloodwork. And with that, you change the way you eat, the way you move, not from guesswork, but from truth."

Esra pictured it. Not numbers on a screen, but decisions that could shift the arc of a life.

"Someone else," the Steward continued, "tracks their diabetes. They share their journey, not for money, but to help. Then an AI notices a pattern . . . something no doctor ever saw."

A flicker of wonder crossed Esra's face.

"You refine it. Share it. And when a researcher uses it to unlock a cure, you're rewarded."

The Steward leaned closer. "You're not selling data, Esra. You're exchanging intelligence."

Esra breathed it in. "Value for value."

"Exactly. And now," the Steward said, "the currency is intelligence."

Esra leaned in. "So, we've been looking at data all wrong. It's also something to build with."

"Exactly," the Steward said.

"Because data can be everything . . . or nothing at all. Its value depends on the moment, the meaning, and your permission."

"So, value isn't just one thing?"
"No," the Steward said. "Value has layers, shaped by what something is, what it can be used for, how it's seen, and what's fair."
Esra let the thought settle. "Then we've been measuring everything the wrong way."

"Yes. And that's why data was ignored. Until now."

He looked at Esra.

"Because now, for the first time, people, not corporations, will decide what is valuable."

Esra whispered, "So . . . we've never actually valued data before, not truly. But now, for the first time, we can."

The Steward said nothing. He didn't need to.

Esra closed his eyes, letting the truth settle.

This wasn't just about value.

It was about everything.

And it was time.

The boy looked around, seeing it all differently now. For the first time, he didn't just know value. He felt it.

But something still lingered in his mind.

"But how do we exchange it safely?" he asked softly. "And what about AI?"

The Steward smiled.

"Patience, Esra."

He turned to the stairwell.

"Some things," he said, "can only be understood from above."

Not Artificial, But Ours

*"We shape our tools, and thereafter
our tools shape us."*

— John Culkin

The door creaked open.
Wind slapped his face, sharp, cold, and honest.
The kind that reminds you, the world won't wait.

Above, the sky stretched, endless and black. Below, the city
pulsed like a living thing.
Streetlights flickered in quiet rhythm, threading between towers
like veins of light.

The Steward followed silently, his cloak catching the wind.
But Esra didn't wait.
He stepped forward alone, not to ask, but to see.

His fingers brushed the stone railing.

"What happens if we get it wrong?" he asked. "What if we build
something worse?"

No answer came. Only the city breathing, machines humming,
neon buzzing, a distant siren's cry.

Esra turned to the skyline.
And something shifted. The buildings weren't machines anymore.
The roads weren't chaos. It was all connected. Patterned. Alive.

This is what they missed; he thought.
The people in the code.
The soul inside the system.

"You feel it now, don't you?" the Steward said.

Esra nodded.
The hum of traffic. The murmur of voices.
It wasn't noise. It was movement.
It wasn't chaos. It was energy.

He opened his eyes and saw not just people.
But potential.

His heart pounded. Something deeply human and electric lit up inside him.

"What is this?" he asked.

The Steward joined him at the edge, clasping his hands behind his back.
"You asked about AI," he said.

"But maybe what you really needed was to see everything first."

He raised a hand.
A glowing thread of data shimmered into view.
It formed a familiar kitchen.

A phone rang.
His mother answered.
Calm voice. Gentle pause.
"I understand the decision."

Another beat.
"But . . . a machine is replacing me?"

"Esra stepped forward, hand outstretched, but the image dissolved before his fingers could reach it."

His hands dropped.
"Why are you showing me this?"

"Because this is where it began."

Esra looked away, jaw tight.
"So that's what happens when the machine decides who matters."

The wind stirred.

"We were told AI would surpass us," the Steward said quietly.
"And so, a few rushed to build something greater than us."

"But why?"

"You've seen history," the Steward replied.

"You stood in the ruins of the past and watched us repeat it,
always chasing, always handing power to the few. And yet . . .
nothing changes."
But never stopping to ask, "Are we losing more than we gain?"

He turned to Esra.
"We need to flip the switch."

The world wasn't waiting for AI to become more human.
It was waiting for humans to see AI differently.

The silence stretched between them
but it wasn't empty. It was full of possibility.

"They'll keep going," the Steward said.
"Faster. Smarter. More efficient. Not because they're wrong,
because they don't know another way."

He looked at Esra.
"But if we don't act soon, we may forget what truly matters."

Esra's grip tightened. "Then we remind them."

A small smile. "Yes. But first, we must change how we see it."

The Steward reached into his coat. A circular device, silver,
almost translucent, rested in his palm.

"What is that?"

"A memory. Not mine. Not yours. But one we need to witness."

He pressed it between his fingers.

The rooftop dissolved.
The wind stilled.
Light bent inward.

And Esra blinked,

A garden emerged.

Soft light filtered through a window.
A man sat on a wooden bench under a tree that hadn't bloomed in years.
He was old. Wrinkled. His eyes unfocused, but kind. In his lap, a device rested.

Beside him, a voice spoke, not loud, not mechanical. Calm. Gentle.

"Would you like me to read it to you again?"

The old man smiled faintly. "Just the part where she laughed."

The voice obliged. And as it did, a memory played, light and warm.

A younger woman's laugh, echoing through a kitchen.
Sunlight on skin. A song playing in the distance.

Esra blinked.

"Is this real?" he whispered.

"It's his," the Steward said. "The memory is his.
The AI had learned his story. Gathered the fragments.
It doesn't just store, it listens. And reminds him who he is."

The old man looked up.

"Thank you," he said softly.

"To be remembered . . . by something that knows me."
He touched his chest. "It makes the forgetting less frightening."

Esra swallowed hard.

This wasn't a machine replacing memory.

This was something holding it gently, so the man didn't have to carry it alone.

He watched the machine pause . . . and wait. Not to move on, but to be with him.

The man closed his eyes.

The moment remained and it always will as it was his.

Alive.

The garden faded.

The city returned.
But it didn't feel the same.
He had seen something pure. Something worth protecting.

Esra's hand trembled against the railing.

"We kept asking what AI would become," Esra said.
"But never what we should become."

"And now?"

Esra's voice hardened.
"AI was never meant to be the hero. We are."

For so long, AI had been framed as something untouchable,
beyond human reach.
But the truth was simpler.

"AI was always meant to work with us," he said.

"Not above. Not against. Not as ruler or competitor, but as a
partner to elevate us."

He exhaled.
"AI should be a companion. Not a master."

The Steward's eyes gleamed. "Now you understand.

"To guide, not decide. To build, not replace."

"AI isn't the future," Esra said. "We are. And it was always meant
to follow our lead."

For the first time, the stranger's words were clear.
AI had become the tool of the few.
Built on data from the many. And in return, people got nothing.
Stories and knowledge never credited. Voices never heard.

Entire nations left behind. "But it's not too late to fix it," Esra said.
"No," the Steward agreed. "The power of intelligence was never
meant to belong to the few. It belongs to all."

"Your own AI. Not a corporate platform. Not something that takes from you but works for you."

"That something," the Steward said, "is yours."

Esra's mind raced.
AI had always felt cold. External.
But this was different.

"An AI . . . that belongs to me?"

The Steward nodded.
"One that learns from you. Protects you. Grows with you."

His own Companion.
Shaped by him.
Grown with him.
Known by him.

A flicker of understanding lit in his chest.
"But where does it live?"

The Steward smiled. "That's a question for another time."

Esra nodded. He wasn't ready for the answer.
But he knew it was coming.

"What about monopolies?" he asked suddenly.

"They'll have to change," the Steward said.

"We can't just break them up. People still need AI."

"They'll still build," the Steward replied.
"But they'll need to open up. Compete. Share.

Even governments will act to prevent power from centralizing again."

Esra nodded slowly. "If everyone had their own AI . . . the old world wouldn't survive."

He turned to the Steward. "Wouldn't it collapse? Wouldn't the companies that built AI fight to keep control?"

"No," the Steward said. "It will evolve.
Because this is no longer about control. It's about potential.
The Steward glanced over the city. "The ones who adapt will survive. Not by owning intelligence, but by supporting it.

Esra considered it.
AI companies as foundations, not gatekeepers.
A shift, not a collapse.

"The world won't stop using AI," the Steward added.
"But trust will define what comes next."

"The ones who build this trust, will thrive."

"Some say the answer is to make AI open," the Steward said.
"Free code. Shared systems."

He shook his head gently. "But that's not freedom. Not if people still don't have the rights to the pieces of themselves that power it."
Esra frowned. "You mean . . . their data?"

"Yes. Their words, their steps, their choices, fed into machines they never got to shape. It's like giving away your voice and never being told who's speaking with it."
He paused, then added, "Freedom isn't just about access. It's about rights. And choice."

And in that moment, he felt it, a flicker of the world he dreamed of.
Closer now. Almost real.

"Then the future of AI isn't just about technology," he said.

The Steward nodded.
"It's about trust.
And trust is no longer given freely."

A new seriousness fell over them.

"There's something else," the Steward said.
He gestured to the city.

The Steward raised his hand.

The city dimmed. The air thickened. Suddenly, Esra stood in the center of it.

A vast, humming plain. Towering data farms stretched to the horizon.

The air was dry. Electric. Heat rose in waves from the metal floors.

Endless processing.

Power consumed without question.

Giant fans screamed overhead. Cables twisted like roots, feeding machines that never slept.

He turned, breath caught.

"This is what powers it?" he asked.

The Steward's voice came from behind him.

"Yes, Esra. AI today is built on more.

More data.

More power.

More storage.

And it's destroying our planet, while remaining out of reach for most."

He turned sharply.

"And is it better for it?"

The humming faded.
The heat dissolved.
Wind returned, cool and sharp against his skin.

Esra was back on the rooftop.
The city pulsed below.

But now, the question wasn't if he would act, only when.

"Tell me, Esra," the Steward said, "would you trust a doctor who memorized every book, but didn't understand the patient in front of them?"

Esra shook his head. "No. They'd miss what matters."

"Exactly.
Intelligence isn't about having everything.
It's about knowing what matters.
But we built AI to devour, not discern."

Esra inhaled. "We consumed everything but understood nothing."

The Steward nodded. "But now, we can change that."

"If we value data," Esra said, "we won't need to store it all?
AI becomes precise.
Targeted.
Respectful."

The wind rose.
Esra felt it, the shift. The choice.

For the first time, AI didn't loom over him.
It stood beside him.

Something for everyone.
Something that could be built right.

"That," the Steward said, "is the real future."

Esra's breath slowed.
"But no AI Companion can be everywhere or know everything."

The Steward smiled. "Which is why we'll need Assistants.
Smaller AIs.
Experts. Focusing on specific things.
Each working with your Companion, not replacing it.

Esra blinked. "What do we call them?"

The Steward gave a wry shrug. "They've been given a name . . .
but it feels mechanical."

Esra grinned. "Then we rename them. Before they become just
another tool."

"Assistants," the Steward said. "Your own team of advisors.
Managed by your Companion."

Then something deeper stirred in Esra.

He turned back to the city, the glow of its lights flickering like stars scattered across the earth. A world shaped by intelligence. A world shaped by people.

Even the name AI felt . . . wrong. Cold.
"Artificial," he muttered. "Like it was never meant to be part of us."
He thought of the man in the garden, the way the machine had waited.
Not to act, but to be with him.
The wind howled between the buildings, but Esra barely heard it.

Because now, he wasn't just understanding it.
He was defining it.
The wind stirred, as if waiting.
He turned to the Steward.
"Collaborative Intelligence. "The words dropped like a stone in still water.

The Steward nodded. "The name was always waiting for someone to see it."

Esra breathed it in.

"It's not just a name," he said.
"It's the reset.
The one we never gave ourselves . . .
Until now."

But he wasn't finished.

"AI is in danger of becoming a product," he said.
"Another cog in the old machine. This time, one that replaces not just work, but us."

His pulse quickened.

"That's wrong."

"We need a new idea.
Something that ensures AI works with us, instead of against us."

He paused, then added:

"Data as an asset ensures that.
If we own the intelligence AI uses, it sets us on a new path."

The Steward's expression shifted, not with surprise, but with pride.

"Collaborative Intelligence isn't just a name.
It's a promise.
And a beginning."

Esra looked over the city again.
This time, it didn't feel distant.
It felt . . . his.
A future still within reach.
If only they were fast enough.

The wind rushed past them.

A mechanical hum split the night.

Esra froze. Overhead, two red eyes blinked into view, drones.

The same kind that had tracked him before.

They hovered, scanning the rooftop like silent predators.

The Steward's eyes narrowed. "They found us."

"Why now?" Esra asked, voice low.

"Because you've changed. And change always draws attention."

The drone lights flashed once, then twice.

The Steward turned sharply. "We can't stay here."

"But . . ."

"Not here. Not yet." He grabbed Esra's shoulder, firm but calm.

"This awakening . . . it's only the beginning. But they won't let it unfold easily."

The wind rushed past them.

The Steward turned toward the stairwell.

"Come, Esra. There's still more to see."

The boy didn't look back.

The weight of everything, the past, the future, the choice, settled within him.

This was no longer a lesson.

It was a turning point.

He stepped forward
not behind the Steward.
But beside him.

Echoes We Buried

"When patterns are broken, new worlds emerge."
—Tuli Kupferberg

The air still crackled with the weight of what had been revealed. The wind howled behind him, wild and urgent, like it didn't want him to leave.

But Esra didn't descend the steps the same way he'd climbed them.
Each step landed with weight, not hesitation, but purpose. The stone felt colder now, but his thoughts burned hotter.
He wasn't just coming down. He was returning changed.

The stairwell spiralled back into the heart of the structure, out of wind and sky, into stillness. With each step, the world changed. Stars gave way to shadow, wind to memory. The rooftop's vastness faded, replaced by architecture and intention.

And then he was there again.

Back in the Gallery.

A corridor of light and shadow stretched before him, arched ceilings, luminous panels, and quiet screens flickering with fragments of knowledge.

The Steward moved beside him like a reflection, cloak whispering across the floor, presence steady.

And then, at the base of the stairwell, she appeared.

Dr. Morgan.
Still. Centered. Waiting.

Her silhouette caught the low amber light of the corridor. Hands clasped in front of her.

She didn't move.

There was a quiet shift in her now. She had always been the constant. The calm.

But tonight, she stood like a turning point, the line between who he'd been and who he was becoming.

Esra stopped, unsure.
After everything he'd seen, he didn't just see a teacher.
He saw a moment he'd been walking toward his whole life.

She smiled gently. But her eyes held more.
A truth not yet spoken.

"Welcome back," she said softly.

Back?

He wasn't sure what she meant. From the rooftop? From this moment? Or from something deeper?

He opened his mouth, but the words didn't come.
The Steward placed a hand on his shoulder.

"Go," he said gently. "You and Dr. Morgan have much to talk about."

Esra hesitated. Then, he followed her.

They walked in silence, their footsteps soft against the corridor floor. The lights hummed quietly above them, the world narrowing to just this moment.

Until Esra couldn't hold it anymore.

"Why did you lie to me?"

His voice cracked open the silence. "You knew. All of this. And you didn't tell me."

Dr. Morgan slowed. For a moment, she didn't turn.
"Tell you what, Esra?"

He stepped forward. "That you knew the answers. That you saw it happening."
She turned. Her face was calm. Too calm.

"Because you wouldn't have believed me."

Esra's jaw tightened. "You don't know that."

"I do," she said gently. "Because you didn't see it, not until you felt it."

"So, you just waited?" he asked. "While everything got worse?"

A pause.

"I didn't say I was proud of it," she said. "But sometimes, knowledge forced too early just closes people off. You had to break through yourself."

He stared at her, fury and understanding colliding in his chest. "You still should have told me."

Dr. Morgan held his gaze.

"We don't have time to argue, Esra.
Remember your dream. Whatever you think of me, remember why we're here.
And that we are helping."

He didn't respond at first. His fists clenched, then relaxed. His breath was heavy, the weight of truth still fresh.
Then he looked at her.

"So be it," he said.
"Then let's make sure no one else has to wait."
Not with blame, but with purpose.

Dr. Morgan gave a small smile. Not triumphant, resigned.
She took a breath. "What did the Steward show you?"

Esra stood taller. The rooftop was still in his chest.
"He gave it a new name. AI. Collaborative Intelligence. We'll have our own. Something we own."

Her smile faded, just slightly. "And how will people even use it?"

Esra faltered. "What do you mean?"

She stepped closer. "The tools are coming.
But the ability to use them . . . that's what we're missing."

Her words hit like cold water.

He nodded slowly. "Then we must. Because this is too much, too fast. If we don't take control, someone else will."

She studied him. And this time, she nodded too.

"Yes. But to change the future, we must change how we learn . . . how we work . . . and how we see ourselves."

She began walking again.

"We've spent too long preparing people to fit into boxes," she said. "Testing them. Grading them. Training them to follow."

Her voice lowered, now more than a whisper.

"We measured success by how well someone could conform.
Not by how much they could create. We never understood the full scope of human potential. The world kept moving . . . but we stayed still."

Esra was quiet. Then, "So what do we need?"

She turned to him. Her gaze sharpened.
A glimmer of fire beneath the calm.

"It's not AI that will change the world, Esra.
It's what we become because of it."

Abilities.

She let the word echo.

"Not just skills. Not test scores.
Abilities. A set of human powers that are uniquely yours."

Esra frowned. "Aren't they the same?"

Her smile curved bittersweet. "If they were, would your mother be where she is now?"

His chest tightened.
The memory struck, his mother with the phone cradled against her cheek, eyes full of something he hadn't understood then, displacement.
Not broken. Just . . . invisible.

She had given everything to a system that forgot her name the moment she logged out.
And no one had told her she could be more than the role she played.
Not even him.

The guilt landed hard. But beneath it, something else stirred.
Resolve.

"Then tell me," he said, voice sharper now.
"What are they? These abilities. I want to know. I need to know."

Dr. Morgan didn't answer. Not at first.
She studied him, letting the flame inside him rise. Letting him stand in it, burn, but not fall.

Finally, she spoke.

"They're not skills," she said.
"Not certificates. Not bullet points on a resumé."

Her voice was steady now, cutting through the fog like truth.

"They're everything you'll need to move through the world that's coming."

She stepped forward.

"Abilities aren't just what we do.
They shape how we see, how we adapt, how we create.
They decide whether we thrive . . . or vanish."

A soft pulse lit the wall panel beside her. With one touch, it flared to life.

Five words appeared.
Skills.
Experience.
Wisdom.
Essence.
Integrative Abilities.

She turned to Esra.

"Skills are what we learn, the tools to apply intelligence in the real world."
"Experience is what we live. It shapes how we understand and use that intelligence."
"Wisdom is what guides us, when to act, how to act, and why it matters."
"Essence is what we bring, the presence, truth, and trust of who we are."
"And Integrative Abilities . . . the power to imagine, adapt, transform, even unlearn."

Esra stared at the words, his voice low. "And we've only been teaching one."

She nodded.

"We taught people to pass. Not to feel.
We tested memory, but not meaning.
We trained for jobs that won't exist . . .
And left people unprepared for the world that is."

Her voice broke, just slightly, then steadied again.

"And when the systems moved on . . . we called it progress."

Esra's jaw clenched.
He wasn't just seeing it now.
He was inside it.

"My mum had experience. She had wisdom. But no one told her they mattered."

Dr. Morgan looked back to the screen.

"That's why we must evolve.
Not just our tools, but our understanding of what makes us capable."

She turned to him.

For too long, we told people knowing enough would be enough."

Her voice lowered.
Harder now. Sharper.

"But the world changed and we left people behind."

Esra's chest tightened.

"My mum wasn't missing intelligence," he said quietly.

Dr. Morgan nodded.
"No.
She was missing the belief she could be more than the role she was given."

A long silence.

"She could have been more."
"She should have been more."

He ran his hand across the glowing screen, words still floating like quiet truths:
Skills. Experience. Wisdom. Essence. Integrative Abilities.

And then, it hit him.

"It was never the technology," he said, barely louder than a whisper.
"It was us."

Dr. Morgan looked at him, but didn't speak.

"You're right, even if we had our own AI," Esra said, "we wouldn't know how to use it.
Not really. Not meaningfully."

He exhaled, the weight of it landing.

"We're not equipped.
We're afraid of losing our jobs, our identity . . .
But that fear isn't because of the machine. It's because we were never prepared to thrive and grow."

He paused, the truth uncoiling.

"We were put in a box and told that was who we were.
What do you want to be when you grow up?
Instead of: What abilities do you need to thrive? What gifts were you born with?"

He paused, then something flickered.
A thought he had long avoided.

"I never fit," he said, quieter now.
"Not really. I was always . . . different."

The memory returned, sharp and unwelcome.
He was twelve. Sitting in the back of the classroom, fidgeting with the corner of a textbook.

"Esra, you're clever," the teacher had said, "but you need to stop asking questions no one's asking. Just stay on track, and you'll do fine."
Stay on track.
Like life came with rails.

"They said I had potential," Esra muttered. "But only if I could be like them. I spent so long trying to be normal. Trying to pass the tests."

He looked up, fire behind his eyes now.

"But maybe I wasn't broken.
Maybe the box was."

He took a breath.

"Now the machine challenges that box.
And instead of rethinking it, we're trying to keep people inside it."

She held his gaze, something soft and fierce behind her eyes.

"Yes," she said. "And now we must change."

He nodded slowly.

"Abilities aren't just what we bring. They're what we've forgotten."

Dr. Morgan turned back to the screen.

"They're not measured on a resumé.
Not unlocked by a grade. They are what make us whole."

Esra exhaled.
And for the first time, he wasn't just listening.
He was seeing. Becoming.

"This . . . this is bigger than I thought."

She smiled.
"Bigger than AI."

He looked up.

"Then where do we start?"

She paused, long enough for it to feel sacred.

"If the old world measured people,
this new one must grow them."

She turned to the screen.

"We start at the beginning, Esra.
With how people learn.
With how they come to know themselves." She touched the final pillar.

"And for that . . .
we must rethink everything we've ever believed about how we learn."

She looked back at him, the glow of the screen flickering in her eyes.

"Because if we don't . . .
the future won't wait for us to catch up."

Michael Clark

Learning to Learn

"We have to recognize that human flourishing is not a mechanical process; it's an organic process."

— Sir Ken Robinson

For a moment, Esra said nothing.

The final pillar dimmed behind them.
Silence followed, not empty but charged.

Esra stood still, the glow of the screen fading from his skin.
Dr. Morgan didn't move.

"To change how we learn," she said quietly,
"I need to remind you of the world that still is."

She looked to her left. A soft nod.

The corridor around them darkened.
Light receded. The walls dissolved, not into code, but into memory.

And suddenly, they were standing at the back of a classroom.

Rows of desks.
Screens flickering in front of silent children.
A teacher at the front, tired eyes and tighter rhythms

Esra's breath caught. "Are we . . . back in time?"

Dr. Morgan shook her head.
"No. This is now. This is still real for most of the world."

She stepped forward, arms folded gently as she observed the room.
"I thought it best you see it this way.
Not as a story. As a living system. One still clinging to life."

The stillness pressed down on him.
He watched a boy blink slowly at a screen, fingers limp on a keyboard.

"We designed it to keep up with the world," she said.
"But the world moved on. And the system . . . stayed."

Esra turned toward her.
"Why are you showing me this now?"

Her gaze remained on the children.
"Because this is what happens when we teach children what to think, and forget to show them the wonder of how to think."

Esra's brow furrowed. "It feels . . . hollow."

"Because it is," she replied. "Designed for an industrial past. Still training people for jobs that no longer exist. Repeating answers instead of awakening minds."

Esra scanned the room. "But there's no one really learning here."

Dr. Morgan nodded. "They're being measured. Sorted. Prepared to compete—but not to create."

With a wave of her hand, the classroom trembled, not physically, but as if waking from a long sleep.

Desks dissolved into vapor. Screens dimmed. Silence cracked.

The walls shifted, breathing into open, fluid space.

In their place, children, walking, building, debating, laughing.

No one sat in rows.
No one waited for permission to speak.

There was no teacher at the front.
Only a presence moving among them.
Not an authority. A facilitator.

Esra's gaze swept the space. "What . . . is this?"

Dr. Morgan smiled. "The world that could be."

Michael Clark

He stepped forward, drawn to the energy, the motion, the freedom.
"Where's the AI?" he asked. "Where's the technology?"

"It's not time for that yet," she said. "Before we learn from machines, we must learn what it means to be human. Our emotions. Our instincts. Our differences. Our creativity."

She gestured toward the children, one helping another, a group questioning, a boy hesitating, then choosing to speak.

"This stage is sacred," she said.
"Because here, we grow the roots."

"What roots?" Esra asked.

Dr. Morgan stepped beside a small group of children, watching them navigate a disagreement, not with argument, but with wonder.

"The roots that anchor us to ourselves," she said softly.
"Adaptability, to bend, not break, when the world shifts.
Curiosity, to explore, not just absorb.
Creativity, to imagine beyond what already exists.
Compassion, to build, not just win."

A pause.

"We cannot download these.
They must be lived."

Esra watched as a girl knelt to help a younger child build something from magnetic blocks.

Another child looked on, absorbing more than instructions, absorbing care.

A memory flickered, his sister helping him build towers of books, long before school made her silent.

"And what about AI?" he asked again. "Surely they need to learn it early?"

Dr. Morgan shook her head.

"Not yet. Not until they know right from wrong.
Not until they can tell what's real and what's noise.
If we give them AI too soon, before the brain is ready, we risk letting the machine shape the mind . . . before the mind knows how to shape itself."

Esra took that in. Slowly.

"So what does the machine do now?"

Dr. Morgan turned to the center of the room. A gentle light glowed in a circle of children, eyes wide and waiting.

"It listens. And when invited, it tells stories."

A soft, shifting voice began to rise from the center. It danced between tones, weaving character, question, and feeling. The children leaned in, enchanted, not passive, but alive.

"This," Dr. Morgan said, "is AI's first role, not teacher, but storyteller.
Not authority, but mirror."

Esra narrowed his eyes.
"It's not giving answers."

"No," she replied. "It's sparking questions.
Awakening their voice before we ever introduce code."

One child raised a hand mid-story, interrupting:

"But why did the character lie?"

The story paused.

The AI responded with a question of its own:
"Why do you think?"

A murmur of reflection rippled through the circle.

Esra's breath caught.

"They're not learning facts," he said. "They're learning to think."

Dr. Morgan nodded, her voice soft but resolute.

"Because if they don't learn how to think . . . they will grow up only knowing how to follow."

"This," Dr. Morgan said, "is where it begins. Before logic. Before algorithms. Before AI is theirs, they must understand their own minds."

She turned to him.

"When the time is right, they will receive their own AI, one that grows with them. One that learns how they learn. One that challenges them."

Esra frowned. "I don't get it."

Dr. Morgan raised an eyebrow, inviting him to continue.

"Yes, they're learning—and it's beautiful. But . . . I still don't see the AI. Where's the real collaboration? Other than storytelling? You've barely mentioned Collaborative Intelligence . . .
How is that?"

She didn't answer right away.
Instead, she turned the question back on him.

"What do you think Collaborative Intelligence means?"

Esra opened his mouth, then paused.
He knew the words.
He'd used them.
But now, under her gaze, they felt unfinished.

"It's people and AI working together," he said slowly.

She nodded.

"True. But that kind of collaboration demands something first."

Her voice steadied.

"It requires us to face a quiet truth," she said, her words like ripples through glass.
"Knowledge no longer lives in our heads. It lives in code, spread across networks, humming in silence."

She paused, letting the weight of it settle.
"And because of that, we must rediscover what can't be copied."

"We must relearn what it means to grow."

A long silence.
"To become the kind of humans capable of bringing what the machine cannot. That's what you're seeing now."

Esra paused, the realization striking deep. Then, with new weight in his voice:

"We kept chasing jobs," he said.
"We trained people to serve systems, then gave those systems to machines."

He looked at the children, not just playing but forming.

"We didn't rethink learning.
We just gave the old model faster tools."

"Exactly," she said, turning back to the children.
"If they don't first learn who they are,
what they value, **how they feel**, what they question,
then AI won't amplify their intelligence.
It will replace it.

And when machines own not just knowledge, but wisdom . . . "
She let the thought hang in the air, heavy as truth unspoken.
". . . we will have given away more than we ever imagined."

"If the world has the courage, we can take another path."
Esra looked at the children, a flicker of belief stirring . . . and a single thought he couldn't shake, what if we don't?

New Partnership

"The fact is that given the challenges we face; education doesn't need to be reformed—it needs to be transformed."

— Sir Ken Robinson

Esra's voice tightened, barely louder than a breath.

"But if we don't get it right . . . if we give up wisdom too . . . "

Dr. Morgan didn't answer. The corridor itself seemed to hold still, as if listening.
Finally, his voice cracked through the silence.

"Then what's left?"

Her gaze met his, steady but heavy.

"We stop thinking," she said softly. "We stop feeling. We stop mattering.

She turned toward the corridor, cool light brushing against the stone. Her steps echoed softly, carrying a weight that wasn't just hers.
"Then let's make sure we don't," she said. "Because now . . . we teach them how to become."

The corridor dimmed behind them. Shadows curled into themselves. The space seemed to inhale.
Walls melted, not into air, but into memory, fragments of the past folding and reshaping, as though even time could be rewritten.

A classroom shimmered into being.
Not dissolved. Evolved.

As the room took shape around them, Esra didn't just watch, he stepped forward, the soft floor shifting under his feet. This wasn't memory. This was motion.

As if the past had stepped aside to let the future unfold.
The children were older now. Nine. Maybe ten.
Their play had become practice.
Their wonder, focused.

They gathered in circles, some debating, some designing, some exploring data from their own lives. Not as statistics, but as stories.

Their learning was no longer general.
|It was personal. And beside each of them, an AI.

Not instructing.
Not dictating.
But reflecting.

Esra's breath caught.
"Finally, they have their own AI."

Dr. Morgan smiled.
"Yes. They're ready."

The AIs asked more than they answered.
Challenged more than they explained.
They adapted, not just to what the children knew, but how they felt.
Their struggles. Their pace. Their voice.

"These AIs grow with them," she said. "They evolve not just from their own data, but from story.
From failure. From resilience."

Esra watched as a girl used her AI to examine her ancestry from her own data, not for grades, but to understand who she was.

Another child explored how their own body responded to different foods.
A third built a simulation, not for a test, but for a question they couldn't stop thinking about.

"This," Dr. Morgan said, "is where Collaborative Intelligence begins to bloom."

He turned toward her.
"Because now they bring something to the collaboration with their data."

She smiled.
"Exactly. They don't depend on AI.
They partner with it."

He watched the room, moved by its simplicity and its power.

"They're not just learning facts.
They're learning to ask better questions."

She nodded.
"And learning how to listen to the answers within themselves."

Esra felt it now.
The shape of something larger.
Not a curriculum.
But a becoming.

The scene shifted one last time. The edges of the room rippled, bending like an old photograph slowly coming into focus, memory stretching toward what could still be.

Esra blinked and time advanced without sound. Now, the children were older, early teens, perhaps.
But the air felt different here. He could sense it in the stillness between movements, in the clarity behind every step they took.

Curiosity had hardened into direction.
Wonder had sharpened into purpose.

Some were crafting intelligence, new models, simulations, tools.
Others explored domains, medicine, architecture, ethics, the arts.
Their questions were sharper. Their skills, more refined.
Their AI no longer just responded. It collaborated.

Each interaction had changed.

It was no longer about learning from AI.
It was about building with it.

"By now," Dr. Morgan said, "they've learned how they learn. They've discovered what fuels them, what challenges them, what makes them unique."

She gestured toward the children.

"Now, they apply it.
Not for exams.
But for life."

Esra saw one child designing a healthcare solution using her family's medical data.
Another building an interactive story world rooted in ancestral mythologies.
A boy debated the ethics of algorithmic bias, with his AI pushing back, presenting counterpoints.

He turned to Dr. Morgan.

"They're not just learning to work with AI.
They're learning how to bring their whole self into that partnership."

Dr. Morgan nodded.
"That is the difference," she said, voice velveted with conviction.
"This isn't education.
This is becoming."

A boy glanced up mid-sentence, unsure of his answer. Esra knelt slightly, offering a quiet nod, not guidance, but permission.
And for a heartbeat, he remembered the boy he once was, waiting for someone to give him that same chance.
The child smiled and continued.

Esra felt it deep in his chest, the kind of knowing that isn't taught but remembered.

"And through that journey," she said, "they grow something even more powerful than intelligence."

She paused.

"They grow essence," she said softly.

"Reputation. Trust. Impact."

The words lingered between them.
"Essence," she whispered, "can't be downloaded. It must be lived."

Esra stood in silence, eyes taking in the unfolding world before him.

"If we do this right," he whispered, "we give them a new foundation."

She met his gaze.
"A journey of lifelong learning," she said, "that never ends."

Her eyes swept the room, the children, the AIs, the questions unfolding like petals after rain."

"No matter what technology comes next, or what the future brings," she added,
"they'll be ready. They'll adapt.
Not because we trained them for it
but because we gave them the roots to grow."

Esra looked on, heart steady.

She nodded too, slow, certain.

And in front of them, children whose potential wasn't measured, but grown.
A world where no one was trapped.
Where wonder was never lost.
Where everyone had the right to reach their potential.

He swallowed.

"But what about the rest of us?"
His voice cracked. "What about those already here?"

Dr. Morgan's eyes softened.

"What about those who weren't given these abilities?" he asked.
"Like my mother. Like millions of others. Is it too late for them?
And . . . what does this mean for work?"

She didn't rush to answer.

Instead, she let the question breathe.

Then

"Ah." A small, knowing smile.

"That, Esra, is the question we've all been avoiding."

She began to walk again, her voice steady but low.

"And now comes the real test," Dr. Morgan said quietly.
"The world won't wait for these children to grow. And if we fail
the ones already here . . . "
She glanced back at Esra, her words falling like a warning.
" . . . everything you've just witnessed will remain only a dream."

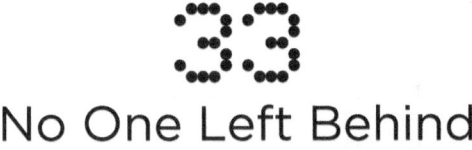

No One Left Behind

"In times of change, learners inherit the earth,
while the learned find themselves beautifully equipped
to deal with a world that no longer exists."

— Eric Hoffer

They stepped into a darker corridor.
The air cooled.
The walls no longer shimmered with promise, they carried a quiet weight now, stone instead of light, time pressing heavier than motion.

Esra followed, more solemn now. The future no longer felt like a distant concept. It pressed in from all sides, real, urgent.

The phrase "no one left behind" wasn't poetic anymore. It was a weight. A reckoning.

Dr. Morgan walked beside him, her steps unhurried.

They turned a corner.
And Esra froze.

The room warped, light bending, space folding, until the scene reshaped around them.

A woman sat slumped against the wall.
Not old, but worn.
Forgotten.

Her eyes flickered toward him, then fell.
Beside her, a machine hummed softly, outdated, glitching, whispering data she couldn't read.

She reminded him of someone.
Not his mother exactly.
But close enough that his breath caught.

"Wait," Dr. Morgan said gently.
"Just . . . watch."

The machine stuttered. Then stopped.
No signal. No guidance.

No AI waiting to guide her. No tools in her hands to even try.
Just a blank gap where help should have been.

He couldn't just stand there. Esra dropped to a knee, reaching
for her hand. It was cold, trembling. She tried to focus on him
but her gaze slipped, like someone half-fading from the edges
of the world.

The broken machine blinked once more, a final message flashing
faintly, "No interface detected." As if the future had arrived for
everyone else but never stopped for her.

"This isn't right," he muttered, sharper now, voice tight with
anger. "Why isn't anyone helping her?"

"All I ever wanted . . . was a way to try."
The whisper was so fragile it felt like it might shatter if he
breathed.
And before he could reply, her presence flickered, the light
collapsing, and she was gone.

His breath came hard, fists clenched, a hollow ache in his chest.
He turned to Dr. Morgan, furious now, not just questioning,
demanding.
"You saw that," he said, his voice breaking. "How can you stand
here and let this happen?

Dr. Morgan's voice barely rose above the silence.
"Her learning never began, Esra.
Because no one ever handed her the tools to try."

Esra shook his head sharply, a step forward, unable to contain
the heat rising in him.

"And that's supposed to be enough? A reason to erase someone?"
The words left him like a fracture too heavy to hold, a vow building in his chest. "This isn't right. It's never going to be right."

Dr. Morgan met his eyes.
"No. But it's real. And it's the future we inherit if we wait too long."

Esra swallowed hard.
The future wasn't distant anymore.
It was unfair.

Dr. Morgan nodded solemnly.
"For us to change, 'no one left behind' cannot be a slogan.
It must be a responsibility.
A repair.
A refusal to forget those already walking this world."

The corridor shifted again, revealing something new. A world of adults. A world still learning.

Some moved with confidence. Others hesitated, watching, uncertain, lingering on the edges. Some stood still . . . as if time had passed them by.

Esra exhaled.

"This is . . . " he trailed off.

Dr. Morgan nodded. "This is where we begin again."

She gestured ahead. "Not all learning starts the same way, Esra. For some, it's about strengthening what they already know. For others, it's about reclaiming what was lost. Abilities dulled by time, like curiosity.

Buried under the weight of outdated systems. And for many, it's about starting from nothing at all."

Esra watched as a man, his hands calloused, his expression etched with quiet frustration, stared at a screen, uncertain.

"For him, data isn't a skill," Dr. Morgan murmured. "It's a locked language . . . and no one ever gave him the key."

Esra's fists tightened. "But how would they know?" His voice caught. "The world forgot to tell them they mattered."

Dr. Morgan looked at him. "That's why your here."

She stepped forward. With a subtle gesture, the world shifted again. The man was no longer alone. Beside him, something flickered into existence. Not a teacher.
Not a screen. Something else. His own AI.

"Not speaking. Not instructing. Listening."

"AI is not here to replace us," Dr. Morgan said. "It's here to unlock potential. To meet each person where they are, not where the world expects them to be."

Step-by-step, the AI built a bridge from what he understood to what he needed to learn.

Esra exhaled. "It's . . . personalized."

Dr. Morgan nodded. "An AI that bends to the rhythm of a person's mind," she said softly.
"Never the other way around."

People at different stages of life, each with their own AI. Some learning in structured bursts. Others learning by doing, patiently, privately.

"This is how it must be, Esra. No two people start from the same place. No two people learn the same way."

A woman in her sixties sat calmly. Her AI beside her, adjusting its pace, not treating her like a beginner, but recognizing the depth of her experience.

"Wisdom doesn't age," Dr. Morgan said. "And it doesn't expire. AI doesn't care about age. It values experience."

She gestured toward the older learners.

"Their data, their lived experience, their insights, their judgment, hold more value than they realize."

Esra frowned. "But . . . do they realize it?"

Dr. Morgan's gaze dimmed.

"Not yet. For too long, the world told them they were past their prime."

She turned as the scene shifted again, slowly, like memory returning.

"But knowledge does not belong to the young alone.
And learning was never meant to happen in isolation."

She gestured to a broader view; groups gathered in learning communities. Conversations flowed. Support thrived. Ideas formed.

"Learning is not meant to be lonely. We grow best together."

Esra watched as a woman mentored a younger learner, her AI enhancing, not replacing, her guidance.

"Mentorship. The bridge between past and future."

She turned to him. "This is the shift. Lifelong learning isn't a task. It's a way of being."

Esra nodded. "So, the world must stop asking, 'What do you know?' and start asking, 'How do you learn?'"

Dr. Morgan smiled. "Exactly."

Then Esra's tone shifted. Sharper now.

"But what about the ones who've been left behind completely? Places where this hasn't even begun?"

Dr. Morgan's voice held steady. "In those cases, AI doesn't assume. It learns with them. It listens, observes, adapts."

"Their journey becomes the data," Esra said. "The compass."

Dr. Morgan nodded. "Yes. And that journey, if we let it, will lead all of us somewhere new."

She gestured again. The world stretched wider. Villages. Remote lands. Places long ignored.

But not as Esra expected. These were not forgotten places. They were vibrant. Alive.

A young girl sat in a rural village, learning from a mobile AI platform, built for her language, her culture, her pace.

"Localized content. This is not charity, Esra. This is inclusion."

She turned to him again. "The world has spent too long calling others 'behind.' What if they've always been ahead, just in a different way?"

And for just a moment . . .
he imagined the Stranger watching.
Not speaking.
Just . . . there.

A faint smile in his eyes.
The kind that says, finally.

Esra turned back, breath steady.

"We're not just catching people up," he said quietly. "We're learning from them, too."

Dr. Morgan's eyes sparkled. "And that, Esra, is how we evolve. Not by pulling others to where we are, but by admitting, we were never at the top to begin with."

Esra stood still for a moment, taking it all in . . . the people, the promise, the world that could be.

Then, finally, he asked:
"But . . . how do they even get access to all of this? The AI. The data. The chance?"

Dr. Morgan's eyes sparkled again, but this time her smile was slower.

"Patience, Esra."

She turned, the corridor beginning to shift once more.

"Some doors must be shown before they're opened."
The corridor seemed to hold its breath, as if the world itself was waiting.
Light shifted, bending softly.
And for the first time, Esra no longer felt like a student.
He felt like a builder of futures yet unseen.

34

Role No Longer Fits

"The illiterate of the 21st century will not be those who cannot read and write, but those who cannot learn, unlearn, and relearn."

— Alvin Toffler

The corridor pulsed with a faint, unreal light, like the future trying to find its shape.
Esra swallowed hard, but his mind had already slipped ahead of him.

The echoes of the learning corridors still shimmered in his memory, fragile and luminous, a promise of redemption not yet claimed.

He turned to Dr. Morgan.
"Then . . . what does all this mean for work?"

A faint smile touched her lips, the kind you see only in the quiet before a truth is spoken.
"Yes, Esra," she said softly. "Your second question."

The world around them began to shift again slower this time, heavy as if weighed down by the future itself.
The air thickened, charged, like a storm gathering but refusing to break.
This wasn't a reckoning of what had been lost.
This was the threshold of what comes next.

Dr. Morgan's voice stayed calm, but each word carried a quiet inevitability.
"In the world that's coming," she said,
"people won't be hired for titles.
No boxes. No shrinking to fit a name on a door.
They'll be chosen for something far greater."

"Far greater?" he snapped, cutting across her words. "You say the future won't judge us by titles, but where was that thinking when the old system discarded people? When the world decided they weren't worth seeing?"

The corridor seemed to hold its breath. For the first time, Dr. Morgan didn't answer immediately, his challenge hanging between them like a weight neither could ignore.

She turned to him, her eyes softer now, carrying a flicker of regret. "You're right," she said quietly. "The old system forgot them. It forgot too many."

Then her voice steadied, sharpening like truth slicing through fog. "That's why the new one must be different," she said.

Her gaze didn't waver now.
"It has to be built on abilities," she continued.
"Because AI doesn't hunt for labels.
It listens for intelligence.
It reaches for insight . . . "

It waits for the human who dares to challenge it, to teach it, to make it more than it is."

The silence stretched, alive, breathing between them.
"For all its brilliance," she continued,
"AI cannot dream.
It cannot doubt.

It cannot ask why until we teach it how.
Without us, it learns nothing worth knowing.
Without it, we stay bound to old limits.
This is not automation.
This is collaboration.

The new world won't be built by job titles.
It will be built by the rarest currency we have,
our true abilities."

The corridor widened before him, endless. But Esra didn't see the strangers passing by.
He saw her.

His mother.
Not bent over a desk.
Not worn thin by a world that had never stopped to notice her.
But standing.
Strong. Certain.

Her face no longer dulled by exhaustion but lit with a clarity
he'd never seen before.
She wasn't surviving.
She was alive in full colour. Her intuition, her quiet brilliance, her
lived experience, they weren't replaceable.
They were needed.

AI hadn't stolen her worth. It had revealed it.

The future wasn't something she waited for anymore.
The future had been waiting for her.

A single tear escaped Esra's eye, hot against the cool air.

A boy's dream, quiet, impossible, fragile, was finally taking shape,
no longer fantasy but something he could almost touch.

Dr. Morgan stepped beside him and said nothing.
There were no lessons now, no grand wisdom to offer,
only stillness, a shared gravity between two souls watching a
new world flicker into being.

"People fear AI will replace them," she said at last, voice barely
a whisper.
"But what if it's the first thing that finally lets them be seen?"

His mother turned to him then, and smiled.
Not a tired smile.
Not the practiced kindness of survival.
A free smile.
A knowing one.

Esra broke. His breath shook as he leaned into Dr. Morgan's quiet
presence, not for comfort but for courage.

And when he finally pulled back, his voice was low, but steady.

"This isn't just a dream anymore," he said. "I'm not watching from the sidelines. I'll make sure this world exists, not just for my mother, but for all of us. No one gets left behind again."

He turned to Dr. Morgan, the weight of a promise in his eyes, steady and unrelenting.
"So if titles no longer define us . . . if what we are is our data, our abilities, even our own AI, becomes who we truly are . . . "

He hesitated, feeling the weight of the question before it left his lips.
" . . . how do we keep track of it all?"

Something in Dr. Morgan's posture shifted, so slight he almost missed it. Like a door long closed had just unlocked.

"Ah, Esra," she murmured, the ghost of a smile returning. "That question may be more important than you know."

Balance Sheet of Humanity

"Not everything that can be counted counts, and not everything that counts can be counted."

— William Bruce Cameron

Esra followed in silence, his mind a storm of questions. If the answer ahead was as important as Dr. Morgan claimed, then it wasn't just an answer, it was a turning point. One that could decide everything.

The corridor grew darker, the hum of unseen currents pulsing like a heartbeat in the walls. At its end, double doors loomed, burnished metal carved with rivers of data and fractured maps of old economies. A single circle glowed at their center, beating slowly, as though the truth beyond had been waiting, not for anyone, but for him.

Esra slowed, his breath tightening.

"If what's on the other side decides our fate," he said quietly, his voice steady but charged, "then someone needs to make sure it's for all of us."

Dr. Morgan glanced at him, the faintest nod of respect in her eyes. She pressed her palm to the circle. The doors answered with a low, resonant hum, light spilling outward. This time, Esra stepped through first.

The chamber unfolded like a planetarium of a broken world. Vast. Circular. A dome of living sky, clouds twisting with constellations that bled into economic charts and shattered trendlines. In the center, a translucent sphere floated, pulsing with veins of light like a mechanical heart keeping score.

But it didn't feel like wonder. It felt like judgment waiting to be read aloud.

Images erupted around him, workers cast aside, wisdom traded for efficiency, lives erased the moment they no longer fit a ledger line. People, millions of them, reduced to numbers, deleted from memory as soon as they stopped making someone else money.

As Esra stepped closer, one of the frozen faces flickers brighter, a woman's eyes locking on his for just a moment.

A sound slips through the static. A whisper.

"Please . . . don't let them forget me."

His breath stops cold. And just as suddenly, she fades again, leaving nothing but the echo of her plea and a hollow ache in his chest.

Esra's stomach twisted.

"Enough," he said, louder this time, his voice raw, cutting through the hum.

He stepped forward, fists clenched, anger shaking his chest.

"Stop showing me this like it's just history. These were people. My mother. Millions like her. And we erased them, not because technology failed us, but because we decided they didn't count!"

The projections stuttered, flickering as if even the room recoiled from his words. Faces froze mid-motion, caught between hope and despair, waiting for someone to see them again.

Dr. Morgan turned slowly. For once, there was no lesson in her eyes. Only weight. Guilt. Regret.

"You're right," she said quietly, her voice stripped of its usual certainty. "It wasn't a game. But the world treated it like one."

Esra's voice trembled but did not break.

"This wasn't technology failing us. This was people deciding who mattered and who didn't."

The projections shivered, frozen faces hanging in midair.

"We built a system that could measure profit to the decimal," Esra continued, stepping closer to the sphere, his words like blows to the silence, "but not wisdom, not judgment, not a single thing that makes us human. And anything you don't count . . . " he glared at the faces around them, " . . . the world erases."

Dr. Morgan bowed her head, shame carved into her features. "We called it progress, Esra. We perfected the balance sheet mentality I warned you about, a century counting only what could be weighed, never what was truly valuable. Experience, insight, even humanity itself . . . vanished because we never gave it a line on the ledger. This was never a technology problem, it's an accounting problem."

Amid the flickering projections, one face takes form he knows too well—his mother's. Not as she was in life, but as the world erased her, faded, labelled "excess cost," a line item waiting to be cut.

Esra stumbled back, breath shaking. "No . . . not her . . ."

He stumbled forward, almost reaching for her fading outline. "She gave everything," his voice cracked, raw and guttural. "And you turned her into a line item to erase."

He turned on Dr. Morgan and Sienna, voice raw, almost broken, "You didn't just erase strangers. You erased her. And every mother, every father, every soul who gave more than your ledgers could measure."

Esra stepped forward again, fire in his eyes now. "This ends with me."

He swallowed hard, rage burning under his skin.

The glowing threads of the ledger twitched violently, stamping names in red, still trying to turn lives into losses.

"This ends now," he said, voice low but unshakable.

The system wasn't just recording history, it was still trying to win.

Esra's fists clenched, rage boiling over.

"No!" His voice cut through the hum, shaking the chamber. "Not again. You don't get to erase them again."

The system flickers, uncertain now, as if for the first time it was afraid of him.

"No more history lessons. Fix it. Show me a world where people aren't expenses on a page."

The chamber pulsed. Light unravelled like threads of memory catching fire. One by one, strands of brilliance stretched across the air, each a life once discarded, now visible. Not liabilities. Not costs. But assets of human intuition, creativity, compassion, and judgment, finally given weight.

Esra's breath hitched. For the first time, humanity wasn't being tallied in losses. It was being seen.

"They're not numbers," he whispered. "They're abilities. The same abilities the old world ignored, the ones that built everything worth having."

Dr. Morgan's voice softened but carried steel beneath it.

"It doesn't matter where you were born, whether you went to university, or if you've ever sat in an office. You still carry value, all of it counts."

Sienna stepped forward; her voice quiet but fierce.

"And in the world to come, businesses won't thrive on efficiency alone. They'll depend on wisdom, empathy, creativity, the things AI cannot generate but needs to grow."

Esra's jaw tightened. "Then we change the foundation."

Dr. Morgan lifted a hand. The sphere flared, a beam of light rising, forming a ledger unlike any ever built. Strands of human essence wove together, pulsing with story, contribution, essence, living proof that people had never been costs.

But as hope flickered in his chest, another truth clawed at him.

Esra's eyes narrowed as the threads of light stretched upward. "Where's the rest of it?" he demanded. "The stolen years, the stolen truths . . . the data they took from us." He stepped closer, voice rising. "It belongs here too.

Where the world can finally see it. Where no one can pretend it's worthless."

Sienna glanced at Dr. Morgan. A reluctant nod passed between them.

"Yes," Dr. Morgan admitted. "For decades, we let empires rise on stolen data while telling people it had no value. We demanded transparency, wrote laws, drafted ethics, but we never put data where it truly counted."

Sienna's tone cut like glass. "Where the world has to see it. Where value is recorded. Where decisions are made."

The sphere responded, a second column of light rising beside the first. Streams of captured moments, signals, lived experiences threaded upward, once invisible, now undeniable. Trails linked data back to individuals, communities, nations. Ownership restored. Value reclaimed.

"No more hiding," Dr. Morgan said, voice hard as stone. "No more pretending it's worthless while empires are built on it."

Esra stepped forward, chest tight with resolve.

"No more pretending," he echoed. "No more throwing us away."

The room seemed to hear him, the ledger glowing brighter, the future leaning toward his vow.

"This is how it should have always been," Esra said, his voice rough but certain. "People first. Data visible. Traceable. Never stolen again."

Sienna's gaze sharpened, words hitting like a verdict.

"Abilities and data aren't just valuable. They're the only advantage left, the one thing no machine can own unless we hand it over."

Dr. Morgan's voice grew quieter, but somehow more powerful.

"The wisdom, insight, and lived experience of people, combined with their data, might one day be more valuable than any business itself."

Sienna's tone softened. "For the first time, we'll value a business not by what it owns, but by who empowers it."

Then Esra saw it, a third column forming beside the others, alive with code and motion.

"Wait," Esra snapped, turning to Dr. Morgan. His voice cracked like a challenge. "Why does AI get a place on this ledger? It's not human."
Sienna didn't flinch. Her gaze locked on his, unwavering, a hard truth on her tongue.
"Because it acts. It decides. It shapes fates," she said, every word cutting the air like steel.
"And whether we like it or not . . . it's a worker in its own right. Power like that doesn't get to hide anymore."

Sienna's voice was steady. "And like every worker, every contributor, it must be seen.
Accounted for. Held to the same transparency we demand of people and data."

Esra's jaw clenched, the thought cutting deep. For a moment, he hated it, but he couldn't deny it. "Then it gets counted too," he muttered, voice hard as stone. "But this time, where we can see it."

Esra stared at the three pillars pulsing before him: People. Data. AI.

His breath trembled, but his voice was steady, unshakable.

"We're finally leaving the industrial age," he whispered. "And stepping into a world where nothing, not people, not their data, not even AI, can ever be hidden or discarded again."

Dr. Morgan's gaze softened, pride flickering beneath the weight of history.

Esra's eyes stayed locked on the glowing ledger, his voice quiet but resolute.

The boy who followed in doubt was gone. What stood in the chamber now was a man forged in grief and fire, no longer asking questions, only making promises the world would have to keep.

"The biggest change in history," he said, voice low but thunderous, "won't be what we invent . . . it'll be what we finally dare to count."

A long stillness. And then, like a promise etched in light, came the first breath of a world that could never go back.

Awakening the New World

"Some revolutions do not shout.
They hum, quietly, just before the world changes."
— Michael Clark

The doors shut behind them, the hum of the balance sheet fading with each step.

Esra walked between Dr. Morgan and Sienna, his thoughts whirling like a storm. Yet something heavier tugged at him now, gravity, not just curiosity.

The door in front of him wasn't like the others. It felt older, sacred, as if every choice humanity had ever made was sealed on the other side.

Veins of light ran through black stone like living circuitry, a heartbeat waiting to be touched.

Dr. Morgan slowed.

"This is the final room," she whispered.

Sienna rested a hand on his shoulder.

"Everything we've shown you has led to this."

At the threshold, the door opened, not with force, but as if it knew him, parting like a curtain of light.

Inside, the chamber stretched vast and circular, silent but alive. The air hummed as if aware of their presence. In the center, beneath a pale column of light, three familiar figures stood.

The Steward, calm, steady as stone.

Dr. Kai, focused, hands clasped as though holding a fragile truth.

Theo—already watching Esra with a quiet, knowing smile.

They weren't gatekeepers. They were witnesses.

The Steward inclined his head.

"These are the last pieces of your journey."

The boy stepped forward slowly, eyes scanning the space. Around the perimeter, glass cases hovered like constellations caught mid-orbit. Inside each one glowed fragments of his journey.

A small village bartered not in goods, but in intelligence, wisdom passing between hands like a shared flame. A classroom shimmered with wonder, an AI guiding young minds toward possibility. An education system stood remade for human potential; its old walls stripped away to make space for what people could truly become. New forms of value glinted nearby, rating models, living licenses—and beside them a personal AI waited in silence, quiet and responsive, ready to serve when called.

At the far edge, the balance sheet of humanity pulsed softly, no longer frantic, but steady, as if the world itself had finally drawn a breath.

And on the walls, images of people across the world, faces he didn't know, yet somehow knew. Their lives were changing because of this place. Because of what they had built.

For the first time, the puzzle wasn't abstract. It was real. It was within reach.

Data, once invisible or stolen, now belonged to people again.

Then his gaze caught on something else.

Floating gently in a glass case behind the three figures was an object unlike anything he had ever seen.

Not large or dramatic, just a shard of possibility suspended in air. Fragile enough to shatter, yet heavy enough to change the world. Esra's chest tightened.

The object pulsed softly, a heartbeat trapped in glass, faint ripples shimmering outward as if the world itself leaned in to listen.

At times it seemed weightless, at others impossibly heavy, as though it carried a thousand untold stories.

Esra's breath escaped in a whisper.

"What . . . is that?"

The Steward's eyes softened. He stepped closer, voice low, almost reverent.

"It's what you've been chasing your whole life, Esra. The truth that defines every one of us, our lives, our choices, our worth, captured for the first time."

He gestured toward the case, the light spilling across his hand.

"For centuries, it slipped through our fingers, stolen, scattered, sold. But this . . . this is the first time we can hold it. Share it. Protect it. A single fragment of a life, bound by permission and truth."

Esra whispered, "Data."

The Steward met his gaze and nodded.

"We call it a token. But it's more than a name. It's the first key humanity has ever held to its own truth, the power to decide when and how the world reaches into what is yours."

Esra swallowed hard, staring at the shard as a quiet weight settled in his chest.

"If that's what a life looks like . . . what have we been letting them take?"

Dr. Kai raised his hand, and one of the other glass cases shifted. The surface flickered, glitching like a broken screen.

Esra flinched. His own face stared back at him, stamped on contracts he had never signed, fragments of his life displayed in places he'd never been, strangers profiting from memories he barely recalled. The sight hollowed him out.

Dr. Kai's voice cut through the hum, steady but sharp.

"This is the world today, your story torn apart and traded like scraps. Every search, every unchecked form, every shadowy click, they built empires from pieces of you. And you never even knew they were gone."

Another glass case flickered beside it, glitching like a broken screen. Esra froze. Staring back at him was that same image from the file, the one he could never shake. His face, but not his face.

The scar, the hollow eyes, the quiet erasure of who he was meant to be. A version of himself rewritten by a world that never asked permission. Esra's hand flew to his temple, fingertips brushing smooth skin, desperate to feel what the image tried to convince him was there. His stomach turned cold, a silent fury knotting in his chest.

Then another case lit up beside it, calm and radiant. Threads of light curled through it, unbroken, flowing back to a single name, Esra. The sight made his breath catch, it was him, untouched, unaltered, whole for the first time.

Dr. Kai stepped closer, voice firm, unyielding.

"And this," he said, gesturing to the glowing case, "is what it could be. Your life whole, untouchable. No one taking it. No one hiding it. Moving only when you choose, on your terms.

You asked how data could be shared, Esra . . . this is how."

He looked up, eyes fierce now.

"This isn't power over you. It's power returned to you."

Esra's breath hitched. He stepped closer, fists clenching.

"So we were never powerless," he said, voice trembling with conviction. "We were just blind."

He stared at the token, voice low but sharp.

"If I share it . . . how will I ever know where it goes?"

"Because it's built on something unbreakable," the Steward said softly. "A living record that remembers every choice, every exchange. Each time your data moves, the world will see it, open, undeniable, unable to be stolen or erased ever again."

Esra shook his head slightly, the weight of it all pressing in on him. "But . . . how can anyone carry this? It's too much. Too complicated."

"Data trusts, Esra."

"Some will help you guard what's yours," Dr. Kai continued. "Stewards for your health, your learning and your very identity. They may carry the weight, but never the right to claim it. It will always be yours, and you'll always know where your life travels, who touches it, and what it's truly worth."

A low vibration stirred beneath their feet, faint at first, then rising. The Steward's face curved into a knowing smile as the floor began to shift, circular panels rotating, unfolding like petals opening to light. A soft, radiant pulse swelled upward.

And then, slowly . . . it rose.

A device, suspended in a narrow beam of blue-white light. Sleek, compact, inevitable. As it rose, a low chime resonated through the chamber—a note that felt less like sound and more like a promise awakening.

The Steward's voice carried through the silence, rich with meaning.

"This is the gateway to your data. And your life."

He paused, letting the moment hold.

"The Super Wallet."

Blue light arced outward, connecting case after case, weaving a living web of light through the chamber.

Health. Identity. Learning. AI. Licenses. Certificates. Insights. Tokens. Every piece of value that had once been hidden or stolen, now visible, connected, alive.

The room pulsed like a heart syncing for the first time.

The air itself felt changed, as though history had shifted its weight.

Esra stared, breath shaking, eyes burning. For the first time in his life, he felt no need to fight for proof of his worth, the world already knew. Everything stolen, everything forgotten . . . could finally be given back.

He swallowed hard, a quiet vow taking shape in his chest.

"This isn't the end of what they owned," he said, voice low but unshakable. "It's the beginning of what we become."

The words didn't just echo. They rewrote the air itself, erasing centuries of silence.

And for a long, perfect moment . . . no one said a word.

When It Touches Your Hands

"Technology is best when it brings people together."
— Matt Mullenweg

Even as his vow settled in the air, Esra felt something stir, not just in the room, but in himself. Possibility had weight, pulling him toward the glass cradle at the chamber's heart, waiting for his touch.

The Super Wallet hovered in its glass cradle. Blue lines pulsed from it like living veins of light, reaching toward the puzzle pieces suspended in the chamber. A system asleep. Waiting.

Slowly, almost afraid, Esra placed his hands on the glass.

The hum stopped. The entire chamber seemed to pause, waiting.

Esra drew in a deep breath as he lifted the case. It rose effortlessly, dissolving into the air above, as if it had only ever been waiting for him.

The Wallet hovered for a moment, then settled softly into his hands. It was warm. Sleek. Smaller than he imagined . . . yet heavy, like it carried something far greater than itself.

A knot coiled in his chest, each inhale a battle he couldn't quite win.

Then, from within, a voice emerged. Calm. Familiar. Like it had always known him.

"Welcome, Esra."

He blinked, stunned.

The Steward's mouth curved into a faint smile. "You once asked where your personal AI would live," he said softly. "Now you know."

The blue veins of light in the room pulsed again, but this time, they pulsed with his rhythm. The chamber synced to him, to his heartbeat, like it finally recognized its true owner.

"This," the Steward said, stepping closer, his voice rich with meaning, "is the gateway."

Esra stared down at the device in his hands, a fragile awe building in his chest. "A gateway to what?"

"To your data," the Steward replied. "To your identity. To your future."

He let the words hang, gravity in every syllable.

"And as for what it does . . . "

The chamber shifted.

The circular walls rippled like glass touched by water. Blue light dimmed, then flared again, threads of energy unfurling beneath their feet, racing outward like the earth itself was drawing a map of his life.

Above, the floating puzzle pieces began to move, slowly at first, then in graceful spirals. They weren't sterile displays or flat icons. They glowed like fragments of a living constellation.

Some carried faint words, truth, choice, family. Others shimmered with blurred images, moments he couldn't quite place, unfinished stories waiting for him to choose how they ended. The pieces expanded and contracted like breathing stars, changing colour in soft pulses, drawing him in.

One rose taller than the rest, a soft silver light spilling from its edges.

Esra pointed, voice tentative. "What is this?"

The Steward gestured. "Your wallet's first connection. We once called them plugins, but that word is too small. These are living bridges, tools you choose to weave into your life."

The panel flickered as if sensing his presence.

"You've already met your first one," Sienna said gently, stepping closer, warmth in her voice.

He glanced down at the Wallet.

The AI. Listening. Waiting. A companion, not a machine.

More bridges lit up around him, glowing in blues and golds.

"AI assistants," Sienna continued. "Specialists for your health, your finances, your learning.
All guided by your companion AI. All serving only you."

Sienna's smile softened, her voice dropping to a near-whisper, like a vow. "You'll never face the world's noise alone again. These bridges listen, they learn you."

Dr. Kai waited a beat before speaking, his voice calm, precise but reverent. "Companies will build bridges too, data trusts, learning streams, personalized services. They won't push themselves on you. You'll invite them, or not. Choice returns to where it always belonged."

Esra moved closer, eyes tracing the fragments as they slowly locked into place, forming pathways, glowing softly with promise. These weren't apps. They were possibilities, each one his to accept or refuse.

His gaze lingered on a new fragment, a vault of light, transparent but impenetrable. Strands of his life flowed through it like liquid gold, protected yet alive.

"You choose your trust," Dr. Kai explained. "You decide what moves, what stays locked, what's seen. Every decision made here, on your terms."

Esra's throat tightened. "All of it connects?" he asked hoarsely. "To the Wallet?"

Sienna nodded. "Yes. Your gateway. Your life. Finally in one place.

For a moment, silence swelled, broken only by the hum of the chamber.

Then his brow furrowed. " . . . But won't this hurt the planet? Running all this?"

The Steward crouched slightly, meeting his eyes, her tone like a patient teacher sharing a long-forgotten truth.

"A question the old world never stopped to ask," she said.

She waved her hand, and a new bridge appeared, energy flows like woven green threads looping through the network.

"These systems breathe," she explained. "They scale when needed. They rest when you do. The future doesn't burn itself out to keep your life alive."

Sienna smiled softly. "Even your wallet sleeps, Esra. It thinks not only of you, but of everything you're connected to."

He nodded slowly, heart pounding with something that felt like hope.

Then his gaze shifted. "What else does it hold?"

The Steward led him toward another display. It glowed gold, silver, deep blue. A quiet, living light.

"This," he said, "is your compass. And your shield."

Symbols floated in the air, truth, kindness, freedom, not just words, but living threads woven into his future.

"Your wallet learns what matters to you," the Steward said. "Not just what you choose but why. It remembers who you are, even when the world forgets."

Scenes formed, him stepping into new spaces, facing unknown systems, but above him, his Wallet glowed, a silent guardian.

"It checks for alignment, for safety, for consent," Sienna said softly. "And if a space doesn't match your values . . . "

"It steps in before you even have to ask," the Steward finished.

Esra swallowed hard. "So, it protects me," he whispered. "Even when I don't know I need it."

A new panel rose, glowing faintly. Inside it, a sealed space. A helix of light floated, delicate yet unbreakable.

His DNA.

His knees buckled, a sob breaking free before he could stop it. Every fear, every sleepless night, every unanswered question . . . it was all here, waiting for him. For once, he wasn't lost.

This was him, his essence. How many times had pieces of this been stolen, twisted, sold without his knowing? And yet here it was, finally, safe.

"This," Sienna said quietly, "is you. Too sacred for anyone else. Not even your AI can see it, only use it with your will."

"All this time . . . " he murmured. "This was me?"

The Steward's gaze held his. "And now, it will only ever be yours."

"What you protect here today can be handed down, untampered, to those who come after you. A truth that outlives us all."

His hand shook as he reached toward the glass, tears stinging his eyes. It wasn't just data being returned, it was his birthright. His dignity. For the first time in his life, he felt like all of him had finally come home.

A new panel rose before him, glowing softly, not a list, not code, but a window into his life finally whole. Threads of light swirled, weaving broken fragments into a single, living tapestry.

"This," the Steward said, "is your Perspective."

Esra tilted his head, watching as moments formed out of light, snippets of his childhood, places he'd been, songs that made him laugh, even the way his friends described him online.

All the scattered pieces that had never spoken to each other now connected, telling a story that felt, complete.

Another shimmer, and a small token formed in the air, pulsing like it had a heartbeat of its own. As it spun, the panel shifted, showing a car, not made of metal and wheels, but of light and memory.

It carried every journey Esra had ever taken as a passenger, the music he loved, the routes that made him feel safe, the times he'd fallen asleep in the back seat and been carried home.

"This token doesn't just hold data," Dr. Kai said gently. "It can create a perspective, a version of you that the world can understand. Today, your life is scattered, forgotten, misunderstood.

But here . . . " He gestured to the glowing car, " . . . your AI can connect every piece, so even a vehicle knows who you are, what you love, what keeps you safe."

Sienna stepped closer; her voice warm. "Perspectives aren't only for cars," she said softly. "They're for hearts too, helping you see what truly matters."

They can shape how you learn, how you heal, even how you find new paths in life. Pieces that never spoke to each other before can finally work together for you."

Esra stared, unmoving. The Wallet wasn't just holding his data, it was life itself, cradling a thousand untold futures, waiting for him to choose.

The chamber seemed to tighten, a silent weight pressing toward him. The others stood silent, as if even they didn't know what he might say.

He looked up at the Steward, voice low but steady.

"Then show me what comes next."

The chamber held its breath, the lights pulsing once, as if the future itself had just taken notice.

Michael Clark

Intelligence We Create

"The moment we see our data as life, not just numbers, everything changes."

— Michael Clark

The Steward's gaze held his, steady and unblinking, voice low and heavy with something older than words.

"To know what comes next, Esra . . . you can't only watch. You have to walk their lives."

The chamber tilted, not with noise, but with gravity and suddenly Esra wasn't standing still anymore. The world bent and reformed around him, threads of light folding space into something alive.

A woman stirred awake, not to an alarm, but to a whisper from her AI.

"Take it slow today," it said gently, syncing with her sleep rhythm, lighting her day with music she'd forgotten she loved.

She opened a small program, not bought from some store, but built by her own hands. Her health, her pace, her choices guiding every line of it.

Esra's stomach knotted. She wasn't being sold to. She was being understood. Not the product, the creator.

Esra's fingers curled against the Wallet, a restless spark in his hands, as if some long-forbidden power wanted to leap free.

He imagined building something for his mother, a small program that would listen when the world didn't, catching her tired sighs and turning them into rest instead of worry.

For the first time, he didn't feel like a passenger in technology's tide.

He felt like a maker.

A second scene unfolded, a teacher on a crowded train platform, her AI glowing softly in her hand.

A nonprofit far away asked to borrow her experience, her learning data, to train a new teaching AI for children who had no schools. One year only. Ethics verified.

She approved, and Esra saw a ripple, her knowledge flowing across oceans, sparking new languages in young minds.

His chest ached. Even the smallest fragments of a life could ripple further than anyone ever dared to believe.

The next image burned bright.

A boy stepped into a car; tired eyes heavy from a long day. But this car . . . it already knew him. It slowed where he needed calm, played the songs that stitched his broken moments back together. It understood because it held his story, not scraped, not stolen, but given with care.

His heart kicked hard against his ribs as the truth took shape before his eyes, human potential, not imagined, but alive.

Not just a thing to trade, but something that could breathe, build, protect, create.

Something they had never seen.

"Show me more," he whispered.

The vision shifted. A young artist stood before a blank canvas, brush trembling in her hand. Her AI didn't scrape. It didn't steal. It asked.

She nodded once, approving the 30-day license for her old sketchbooks.

Golden threads of light wrapped around them, safe, trackable, returning value to her with every future stroke.

Then she looked up.

Her eyes found his, as if the space between worlds had thinned.

No words passed, only a small, quiet smile.

Not just gratitude, but recognition.

As if to say, this is what we were meant to have all along.

This wasn't code. It wasn't a currency. It was a piece of being, finally set free.

His fingers tightened around the Wallet. The thought burned through him like fire: If this is what data can do . . . what have they been taking from every life, every moment, all this time?

He spun toward the others, pulse hammering. "And what if this goes wrong? What if the world isn't ready, if people aren't ready? Isn't this just handing fire to a crowd that's never seen flame?"

"Esra, power doesn't disappear just because you hide it," Sienna said softly, but her words cut through the air like glass. "It only ever shifts to someone else. And we've lived under that shadow long enough."

Dr. Kai's words arrived unhurried; each one chosen as if tested before release. "The real risk isn't giving people control. It's letting them live without it, forever."

The Steward's gaze swept the chamber, his voice quieter, weightier, as though speaking to the future itself. "This isn't just a tool, Esra. It's a turning point. The question isn't if we can handle it . . . " he locked eyes with the boy. " . . . It's if we can afford not to."

Esra's throat burned as the weight of choice pressed heavier than the Wallet itself. This wasn't just about building apps. It was about rewriting how the world worked, and wondering if humanity deserved a second chance.

The chamber brightened, threads of light swirling back toward him, pulling every vision into the center of the room, into his hands. The others stood silent. Even the chamber seemed to wait.

He looked at the Wallet, then up at them, breath steady now.

"And yet . . . " his words landed like a fragile truth breaking free. "I need to believe we're ready."

The words cut through the stillness like a spark in dry air.

"But if one life can do this . . . what happens when the whole world wakes up?"

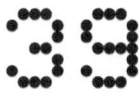

Where Light Breaks Through

*"Even the darkest night will end,
and the sun will rise."*

—Victor Hugo

The hum faded. The panels withdrew, dissolving like mist kissed by morning light. The glow softened, not from above, not from below, but from the room itself. And from within Esra.

He stood still, the power of his own words still echoing in the chamber, like they were alive, refusing to vanish. No more screens. No more panels. Just him and the Steward.

Esra looked around, eyes adjusting to the stillness.

It was quieter than silence, a pause that seemed to ask him what came next.

The Steward's voice broke through, steady yet weighted with something older than words.

"You've seen what's possible, Esra. But this is only the beginning. What comes next . . . will feel like the world turning inside out, but in truth, it's finally turning right side in."

Esra swallowed hard. His chest burned, not with doubt about himself, but with questions too big to ignore.

"What if the world isn't ready? What if people still choose the same shadows we've been living in?

What if everything I've seen here . . . never makes it beyond these walls?

He glanced at the Wallet in his hands, its glow pulsing like a heartbeat.

For the first time, it didn't just feel like hope, it felt fragile.

As if the future could still slip through his fingers and be lost forever.

The Steward stepped closer, eyes narrowing with a weight Esra hadn't seen before.

"Then," he said slowly, each word a warning,

"We may already be too late."

Esra's breath caught.

The words landed like a prophecy, turning his earlier belief, that maybe they were ready, into a challenge, a dare he wasn't sure humanity could meet.

Esra's pulse thudded in his ears. For a long moment, the weight of the Steward's words sat heavy between them, like the future itself was holding its breath.

He finally lifted his gaze, eyes burning with a mix of defiance and desperation. "Then why me?" he asked, voice sharp, cracking on the last word. "Why give this to me if the world might still choose wrong?"

"Why let me see all this if it's already too late?"

The Steward didn't move, didn't flinch.

His silence felt deliberate, as if he was leaving space for Esra's own truth to surface.

Esra clutched the Wallet tighter, its weight a question mark pressed into his palms.

"I thought this was just my dream," he whispered, each syllable scraping out of him like a confession. "But it wasn't, was it? It wasn't for me. It was for all of us."

He looked up sharply, eyes meeting the Steward's with something fiercer now.

"If I walk out of here and nothing changes, then what was the point of choosing me?

Was it just to watch the world burn slower this time?"

The room seemed to tighten around his words. Even the threads of light along the walls flickered, pulsing in rhythm with his anger, his fear, his desperate hope that there was still a way forward.

The Steward's face softened, not pity, but something closer to recognition, as if he'd waited for this moment. "No," he said quietly, "you weren't chosen to watch. You were chosen because you're the only one who's ever asked that question."

A faint pulse stirred in Esra's pocket.

He froze.

The book.

His hand slipped inside, fingers brushing its worn cover.

He hadn't thought about it in hours, yet now it felt warm, alive, as if it had been listening to this whole time, waiting for this moment.

He drew it out slowly.

The cover glowed faintly in the chamber's light, and for a heartbeat, he could swear it breathed.

A page flipped open on its own, revealing a single line he didn't remember reading before, "The future waits for the ones who dare to hold it."

His chest tightened.

It wasn't for him. It had never been just for him. This book had carried the history they'd lost, but also, a promise, a promise meant for everyone.

He looked up, eyes meeting the Steward's.

"It's not mine," Esra whispered, voice rough but certain. "It's theirs. All of it."

"Maybe the world was never ready," Esra continued, his voice steady. "Maybe it never will be. But we can't wait for perfect to start."

The words surprised even him, but once spoken, they settled in the space between them, too heavy to take back.

The Steward nodded once, and with a slow, deliberate gesture, he extended his hand toward the far side of the room.

A door shimmered into being, not mechanical, not ancient, but as though the world itself had decided to make space for what must come next.

Threads of light bled from its edges, stories, patterns, lives, woven and waiting.

From his coat, the Steward withdrew something small, glowing, shifting like thought made solid, alive in his hand, a memory key holding everything he had just witnessed, waiting for him to carry it forward. He placed it in Esra's hand, closing the boy's fingers around it.

"Because the future cannot be built with the same hands that once locked it away," the Steward said softly.

"And now, Esra . . . it's in yours."

Esra took a step, the glowing memory key burning warm in one hand, the book clutched in the other. For the first time, he didn't feel like a boy being led, he felt like someone finally returning to where he was meant to be.

The doorway widened.

Light gathered, not harsh, but soft, like memory finding its way home.

And waiting beyond it, on the other side, were all of them.

The Steward.

Sienna.

Dr. Kai.

Theo.

They weren't there to lead him anymore, only to stand back, knowing the next step belonged to him alone.

Esra stepped out into the open air.

Neon lights still bled through the rain-soaked streets in the distance, the skyline still hummed with static and noise.

But beyond it all, past the endless flicker of distant billboards and the darkness of the hour, there was a brightness.

A fragile light cutting through the downpour, a promise the city had forgotten it could keep.

For the first time, Esra didn't just see the city as it was, he saw what it could become.

He glanced back once.

The observatory behind him no longer felt like a chamber.

It was a bridge, not to somewhere far away, but to what must come next.

The Steward came to stand beside him, voice barely above a whisper.

"Remember why you began this, Esra. You know what they've taken. Now you must finish what you started, not for you, but for all of us."

The words sank deep, heavier than the glowing device in Esra's hand, heavier than the dream that had followed him this far.

Esra stared at the horizon, the weight of choice pressing heavier than ever. Some truths refused to sleep until they were set free. He drew a slow, steady breath, eyes locked on the faint glow beyond the rain-soaked skyline.

"If the world burns again . . . " His eyes hardened, unblinking. " . . . it won't be because I stayed silent."

The Steward gave a single nod to Theo. "He'll take you back."

Theo opened the car door, waiting silently.

Esra turned once more toward the others, the wind carrying something invisible between them, possibility itself, fragile yet unstoppable.

Their eyes met. No words needed.

Esra held their gaze, a single thought blazing louder than the storm around them:

Some truths can be buried, chained, denied, but not forever. Not anymore.

PART 5

A New Beginning

40
Road That Remembers You

"And the end of all our exploring will be to arrive where we started and know the place for the first time."
—T.S. Eliot

The car door closed with a soft click, and as the engine hummed to life, the horizon ahead seemed to tremble, like the first line of a story finally being written.

They pulled away, the observatory dissolving in the rearview mirror, not vanishing but slipping out of reality, like a dream refusing to admit it was over.

For a while, there was only the road.

And the silence. Not the kind that asks to be filled, but the kind that lets the soul rearrange itself.

Outside, the world moved. But inside the car, time stretched.

Slowed. Settled.

Esra sat still, one hand resting on the memory key in his palm, the other on the worn book against his chest. Symbols, truths, choices, all of it humming through him like a second heartbeat.

Theo glanced sideways, voice low. "Heck of a journey."

Esra didn't answer at first. Just nodded, as if the words hadn't reached him yet, as if he was still catching up to who he'd become. "I don't know if I'm supposed to feel excited . . . " he said finally, voice quiet but steady, "or terrified."

Theo gave a faint smile.

"Probably both."

The car rolled on, highway lights blurring like the last pages of a book turning too fast.

Theo glanced over; his voice softer than Esra had ever heard it.

"Does it still feel like a dream?"

Esra blinked, his throat tight. "No," he said slowly, eyes on the rain-smeared glass.

"It feels like . . . a beginning I don't know how to live yet."

Theo let out a breath, almost a laugh, but heavy with understanding.

"None of us do, kid," he said, his gaze fixed on the endless road ahead. "But maybe beginnings don't need instructions." Esra's hand found the book, pulling it free as if on instinct.

He didn't open it this time. He just held it, feeling its quiet pulse, and for a long moment, it felt like they were both holding the same thought, that the story of what came next wouldn't be written alone.

Outside, the city began to bleed into view.

The sky was still dark, rain dripping from neon signs, but something in it felt different.

Billboards flickered with static, then glitched for half a second, a phrase pulsed through the noise, "Truth wants to be free."

Windows in far-off towers glinted strangely, as though the night itself had shifted its gaze.

Esra felt it. The city wasn't awake yet. But something in it had stirred.

He leaned forward slightly.

"Can you stop here?"

Theo didn't ask why. Just nodded. The car slowed, tires whispering against wet pavement.

They pulled to a quiet stretch near the city's edge. The skyline blinked uncertainly in the mist, half the old world, half something waiting to be born.

Theo turned to him. "You sure?"

Esra nodded once. "I need to walk." Theo hesitated, fingers still resting on the wheel. His voice came low, rough around the edges.

"I knew you had it in you," he said, not as praise, but as fact, as if he'd seen this ending before Esra ever did. Esra swallowed, words catching in his throat. There was so much he wanted to say, and none of it enough.

So instead, he just met Theo's gaze, letting gratitude pass between them like a silent pact. Theo gave the smallest nod, a quiet pride in his eyes.

"Go on, kid," he murmured. "The world's been waiting for someone like you to wake it up."

He opened the door. The wind met him, damp and restless, carrying the scent of rain and distant electricity. Overhead, faint at first, a low mechanical hum drifted through the mist.

Esra glanced up. Drones, sweeping the skies, searching.

Not for just anyone. For him. Theo caught his look, his own face sharpening.

"They know you're awake now," he said quietly.

"Don't let them put the world back to sleep." Theo's eyes met his one last time.

Not as a driver.

Not as a guide.

But as a witness, to a boy who was now something more.

The door closed softly behind him.

Theo's tail lights faded into the wet haze, swallowed by rain and distance, leaving Esra alone with the city.

He walked, steps slow, deliberate, each one sinking into the rhythm of a world that hadn't changed, yet somehow already had.

He turned a corner. Beneath the steel arch of a tower still branded with a data empire's logo, a figure waited.

Still. Composed. Watching. As if he'd always known Esra would come.

As if he'd been waiting all along. Above, a low mechanical hum sliced through the mist.

A drone swept overhead, its searchlight cutting a cold line through the rain, pausing just long enough to mark him in its beam.

Not hostile, not gentle, just a reminder.

The world he'd glimpsed in the observatory hadn't arrived yet.

The old one was still watching.

And just before Esra stepped forward, he remembered his dream, that flicker, that single voice whispering through time,

"One person can change everything."

And maybe . . .

Just maybe . . .

That person . . .

Was him.

41
Conversation with Doubt

*"All that you touch you change. All that you change changes you.
The only lasting truth is change."*
— Octavia E. Butler

The wind stirred. Not strong. But certain. Like it knew something was about to break.

The city held its breath. And Esra stepped into it, not with fear, but with the weight of what he now carried.

Above, the drone hovered. Its searchlight tracked him like a question, illuminating the cold, wet street below. As if to say, This is the moment. Choose wisely.

Ahead, the shadows parted just enough. A steel archway cut through the rising light, casting long lines across the pavement like fault lines. And beneath it, a figure. Still. Composed. Watching.

The beam widened. Now they both stood in its circle of light. The rest of the world, cloaked in shadow. Only they remained, the past and the possible, face to face.

Behind the figure, a tower rose. Glass and gravity. A monument to the old world. Its logo, once worshipped, now weathered, caught the morning like a dying star. Flickering. Fading. Still dangerous.

"Simon," Esra said. It wasn't a question, it was recognition. "You followed me."

Simon stood motionless. Like stone. "I never left," he said. "I'm the part the world still listens to."

The air thickened. "You think this will work?" Simon asked, voice cold, surgical. "Personal AIs. Wallets. People managing their own systems?" He tilted his head, one eyebrow lifting in disdain. "They don't want control, Esra. They want comfort. Easy. This is too much. Too soon. The infrastructure isn't ready, and it never will be."

Esra didn't flinch. "You're right," he said. "Yesterday, it wasn't ready. But this isn't yesterday."

He stepped closer. "AI changed the rules. We're not replacing the system. We're unlocking the person."

Simon's eyes narrowed. "And the companies? The ones that feed on silence and scale?" He advanced a step. "You think they'll just . . . let go?" He didn't wait for an answer. "They'll fight you. Every inch."

Esra stood his ground. "This isn't about power," he said. "It's about potential. Power won't vanish. It'll rebalance. Those who build trust will still thrive, maybe more than ever. But this time, we rise with them."

Simon shifted. His shadow stretched like a threat. "You give people too much credit," he muttered. "They don't care about data. They scroll. Click. Surrender it without a thought."

Esra moved forward. "They don't care about data. But they care about their kids. Their choices. Their health." He met Simon's stare. "When they understand what data really is, they'll care."

Simon folded his arms. Something hardened in his jaw. "Tokens. Licenses. Trusts. It's too complicated. You'll lose them before you've started."

"It's only complicated because no one ever made it simple," Esra replied. "Until now."

Simon's voice dropped, low, almost bitter. "This is a dream. A utopia written in poetry. You're asking people to believe in something that's never been done."

Esra nodded once. "That's what every first chapter sounds like." He raised his chin. "Dreams aren't fantasies. They're futures, waiting for someone to choose them."

Michael Clark

Simon hesitated. His next words came slower. "Why would you want this? The friction. The failure. The blame?" He gestured toward the tower. "You could walk in there tomorrow. Sign your name. Forget your data. Live soft. No resistance. No risk."

He turned to the street. The city was waking. Faces lit by screens. Swiping. Laughing. Tuned in. Tuned out. Happy.

"Look around, Esra. They've already chosen. Comfort over complexity. Ease over effort. Tech runs their lives, and they like it that way."

Simon stepped closer. His voice sliced the air.
"They don't want more control, Esra. They want less responsibility."

The words struck deep. Sharp. Real. A final test.

Esra stood still. His breath caught. He almost listened.

"No one would blame you," Simon said. "You're just a boy with a story. Let the world spin. You got further than most."

Silence.

Esra closed his eyes. Not to escape. To remember.

A whisper in the dark. A hand on his shoulder. A warning in the Stranger's eyes, "If we miss this moment, we don't just fall behind. We fall apart."

Then he saw her, his mother, budgeting in the dark, forgotten. A world spinning fast, but leaving too many behind. The Steward's voice, pulling at his heart, reminding him why he began . . . and why he had to finish. And Theo's face when he closed the car behind him.

Not ghosts. Anchors.

All this was his dream. Our hopes. In his hands.

His eyes opened sharply. A low mechanical hum returned, closer now. The drone descended from the mist. Silent as judgment. It hovered between them. The spotlight narrowed.

Esra froze, rooted to the spot, as it scanned his face. Then a beam bent, projecting an image onto the wall behind.

His face. But not the one standing here. The version from the file. Branded. Broken. A scar across his temple. Eyes hollow. Soul edited.

Simon didn't react. The drone was part of him. Part of this place.

But Esra did. His breath locked in his throat. The world tried, one last time, to tell him who he would become.

He reached into his coat. The book. And with a swift, defiant strike, he smashed it into the drone.

Sparks flared. The image shattered. The drone reeled, light flaring, then dimming. And then, it rose. Back into the sky. Gone.

Esra growled at the sky. "Don't tell me who I'll become." His voice cracked, not with fear, but fury. "Not you. Not them. Not ever again."

Simon watched him. Emotionless. Not as a sceptic. But as something else.

A long pause stretched between them. He finally spoke, quietly. Almost robotic. "Interesting. You've changed."

Esra looked at his hands. Not with power. But with proof.

He stepped forward, now in darkness. Only the neon lights of the city glowed across his shoulders.

"You're right, Simon," he said. "It's hard. Risky." He exhaled. "But the cost of doing nothing . . . is everything."

"I'm not here to win a debate anymore. I'm here to rewrite the story."

Simon's stare didn't break. "They don't care, Esra. They never have."

"They will," Esra said. "Because they care about life. And data is life. It's who we are."

He stepped closer. "And if we want a future that's truly ours . . . we start with what makes us human."

Simon's voice lowered. "You? Now? You think you can do this?"

Esra touched the book beneath his coat. The memory key pulsed in his other hand.

"Why not me?" he said. "Why not now?"

His fingers pressed to his chest. Over the beat. Over the data inside.

"We have everything we need, protection, purpose, a mirror that finally shows who we are. And for the first time . . . we're looking."

"We don't have to fight the old. We evolve into the new. One voice won't change the world. But one choice can."

Simon said nothing. The wind moved through the archway like a warning.

Then, "There's no global framework for this," Simon said. "No rules to hold it."

"Then we build it," Esra replied. "Brick by brick."

Simon gritted his teeth. "No one will give us permission."

Esra's eyes narrowed. "Change never asked for it. Law follows culture, Simon. Not the other way around."

Simon exhaled. Rough. Tired. Real.

"They won't thank you, Esra. Not when it gets hard. Not when it breaks what they thought was safe. You'll be blamed before you're understood."

"I know."

Simon's voice softened, just slightly. "I'm not your enemy," he said. "I'm the voice that held the center while the world spun." He looked away. Then back. "You silence me . . . and everything gets louder."

But this time, he didn't resist. He listened.

" . . . You really believe they're ready?"

Esra turned. Looked at the city. Its pulse. Its chaos. Its unfinished story. Then back at Simon

"No. But belief isn't what makes us ready. Action does."

Simon inhaled. Deep. Measured. A breeze stirred.

Simon walked toward Esra. Face to face for the first time. His expression hardened, not softened. A last defence building behind his eyes.

He looked like the future, if no one stopped the past.

Not villainous. Not monstrous. Just . . . precise.

Everything about him, engineered for function, nothing wasted on warmth.

Posture: perfect. Presence: quiet. Purpose: undeniable.

A man who built the world's systems, and forgot the people inside them.

Efficiency over empathy. Scale over soul.

He wasn't here to fight. He was here to hold the line.

The industrial mind, made flesh.

"You think this world will follow you just because you showed up with conviction?" His voice was low now. Controlled. "They'll laugh first. Then they'll tear it down."

He took a step forward, almost defiant. "And when they do . . . you'll stand there wondering if any of it was worth it."

Esra met him, unwavering. "Then I'll stand there anyway."

Simon exhaled. Rough. Like the air had turned against him. He looked toward the rising city, flickers of movement returning to life.

Then, quietly, giving something up he never thought he'd lose, "If the system falls . . . I don't know what holds us together."

He didn't wait for Esra to answer. A long silence.

Then, finally, "Go," he said. Not gently. But with weight. "Let's see if the world remembers how to dream.

The words hung there. Not a blessing. Not forgiveness. A dare.

Simon held Esra's gaze a second longer. Then something . . . shifted. Not in his tone. Not in his stance. In his form.

It was subtle at first. A flicker at the edges. Like light struggling to hold him in place.

His outline glitched. Sharpened. Softened. And Esra understood: This version of Simon wasn't flesh and bone. He was logic. Doubt. History. A guardian of the old world, finally letting go.

The glitch deepened, until Simon's figure faded into static. And then, nothing.

Only Esra. The arch. The city ahead. And the future he had chosen to meet.

Michael Clark

Our Moment

> *"The world is changed by your example,*
> *not by your opinion."*
> — Paulo Coelho

Simon was gone. Not defeated, released. A question exhaled, finally let go.

And Esra stood where doubt had once stood, beneath the arch, before the city.

The skyline loomed, unchanged in shape or light, but the air felt different.
Like something massive had just exhaled.
The chaos felt slower now. The noise less certain. As if the world itself had paused . . . to think.

Esra walked quietly, the streets whispering beneath his boots.
In his hand, the book pulsed gently warm, steady. Its spine marked by the fingerprints of a journey only he could have taken.
Tucked into the back cover, the memory key. Still humming with everything he had seen. Everything still to come.

Above him, the moon hung low, full and watchful, trailing behind like a quiet guardian.
It didn't blink. It didn't ask questions.

Esra turned onto his street. Each step felt quieter than the last.
The world didn't shout anymore. It listened.

And there, waiting beneath the soft glow of a flickering streetlamp, stood the Stranger.
Same coat. Same posture. Same stillness.
Only now, Esra didn't feel small.

He stopped at the base of the steps.
"Why are you here?" he asked quietly.

The Stranger didn't move.
Then he spoke.

"To witness the boy become who he was always meant to be."

This wasn't a test anymore.
It was something else. Like a torch being passed. Or a final mirror held up.

Esra stepped forward.
His voice lower now, almost to himself.
"I used to think I was supposed to fix the world."

He looked down at the book in his hands.
"The truth is . . . it was never my dream."

He looked up again. His eyes steady.
"I was just the one who could carry it. The one who could give it form.

The Stranger blinked slowly.
Like stone cracking for the first time in centuries.

"I chased knowledge," Esra continued. "I hunted answers. I thought that's what power was."

A pause.

"But the book taught me to listen. The observatory taught me to see. And the people . . . they taught me that none of this matters unless it's shared."

The Stranger shifted his weight. Not a gesture of impatience. Of gravity.

"This wasn't about a platform," Esra said. "Or a protocol. It was about remembering who we are."

He looked at the memory key, then at the Stranger.
His voice softened, edged with curiosity.
"That text message . . . was it you? And did you write this book?"

A pause. Then a smile that felt strangely familiar, like looking at a future self that had already made peace.

"It's yours now." A beat. "And theirs."
He nodded to the skyline.
"To everyone."

Another silence. Then:

"You needed a story to follow. Until you remembered it was yours to write."

Esra smiled faintly.
"That's the thing, isn't it? We wait for someone to give us the answer. But maybe the only real answer . . . is to begin."

The Stranger returned the smile, this time with something deeper behind it.
"It was never about the system," he said. "And it was never about the book."
He looked at Esra, almost gently.
"It was to remind you that we can choose. That we still can. That we must."

He paused. Then, slowly, reached into his coat.
From its folds, he drew out the Super Wallet, its surface glowing like something alive.
"You might need this."

Esra blinked.
"But how did you . . . ?"

Esra took it.
Carefully. As if holding the weight of a future not yet born.

"I'm not the smartest," Esra said. "Not the strongest. I was just the one who didn't look away."

"And that," the Stranger said, voice low and deep, "is how change begins."

Esra looked around them.
The flickering streetlamp. The quiet city. The book. The wallet. The memory key.

"I thought I was alone."

"You were," the Stranger replied. "And you weren't."

Esra stepped in close.
"Will I ever see you again?"

The Stranger tilted his head. The streetlight caught his face just long enough to glimpse a shadow of something else, something older than time, and far more human.

Then he spoke, voice soft but sure:
"You were never meant to follow me."
"You were meant to lead."

And then he was gone, swallowed by the shadows, like a question finally answered.

Esra wasn't lost anymore.
The seeker had become the guide.
The question had become the answer.

Esra stood in stillness. Not in fear. Not in doubt. In knowing.

He looked down at his hands. Once, he thought the rules were broken. But they weren't. Just unfinished.

He turned one palm upward, and watched as streams of soft light traced across his skin, like circuits made of memory. Like identity made visible.

Not power.
Proof.
Proof it was there, waiting, in everything we've lived.
That's what data is, he realized. Not numbers to be mined. But memory, meaning, and self, deserving of care, ownership, and purpose. A true asset.

He looked up.

The girl in the yellow coat. She stood beneath a street mural, the same spot she once danced.

He remembered now, how she first appeared like a glitch, near the bookstore, just before it all began.
When the world was still noise, and she flickered like a glitch.
No longer a metaphor.
A message.

She looked at Esra, eyes bright, anchored in something new.

Hope. And she smiled.

Like hope made flesh.
Like the next generation saying, Thank you for seeing us. Thank you for remembering.

Esra nodded back, barely a motion.

But enough.

A door behind him creaked open.

He turned.

And there she was.

His mother.

Not restored to a past version. Not the woman the machines had replaced. But the woman they had forgotten how to see.

She didn't speak.
She didn't need to.

He walked toward her. Slowly. Deliberately.

For a moment, they just stood there.

Then he held out the book.

And she held out her hand.

It wasn't about restoring what was lost. It was about valuing what remained.

A child passed Esra, catching the glow of the book.
An old man paused, sensing something in the air.
Two strangers crossed paths and, for the first time, looked up from their screens, and truly saw each other.

Esra turned to them.

Not from a stage.
Not behind a screen.
Just . . . as himself

Everything around him, AI, the outdated systems people feared, none of it was the enemy.
Not if people chose to use it differently. To ask more of it and of ourselves.

He asked softly:

"What if your story was valued?"
"What if we stopped building digital walls, and started building with each other?"
"What if we chose to learn differently, and used this moment to evolve, instead of just struggle . . . or blame the technology?"

They listened.

One person took out their phone. Then another.
Not to scroll.

But to ask.
To share.
To learn.

And maybe this wasn't just a message for them.
Maybe it was for all of us.

What if the future isn't waiting for answers?
What if it's waiting for us to ask a different question?

A voice rose from the crowd.

"Then what do we do next?"

Esra looked out across them.
A sea of people, finally awake.

For a moment, he didn't answer.
He just breathed, taking in the light, the silence, the stillness that felt earned.

And he thought:

We used to worry that AI would replace us.
But maybe it wasn't the machines.
Maybe it was us, forgetting who we are, and who we could become.

Now . . . we remember.
Now, we begin again. Together.

He smiled, steady now.
Not as the boy chasing answers.
But as the one who finally remembered.

He was never meant to fix the world.

He was meant to remind us that we could.

Esra looked to his mother for approval.
She gave a small nod, not dramatic, but enough.
He turned. His voice, quiet.
Certain.
"Whatever comes after . . . we build it. Together."
"We have the tools. We just need the will."

Not everyone would say yes.
Some would scoff.
Others would resist.

But change doesn't wait for comfort.
It comes when it's ready.
And stays when we are.

The city didn't stop. But it trembled. It shifted.

Far away, screens flickered.
Not with noise, but with attention.

News feeds bent at the edges.

And in corners of the world Esra hadn't touched, people began to speak up.
Not all at once. But enough.

One by one, lights flickered on in the buildings around them.

Signals of people reconnecting with purpose.

And somewhere beneath it all, not from machines, but from people, came a new kind of hum.

A sound built for connection.

As Esra stared out, a camera would rise, watching him, the street now alive with possibility.

Behind him, the skyline pulsed, not with noise.

With rhythm.

He paused for a breath.

Smiled, softly, not for what was behind him,
But for what lay ahead.

Because this time . . .

He had something to give back, we all do.

And from above, the moon watched it all.

As if it always knew:

We were never lost.
We were just waiting for someone to remind us how to begin again, how to think differently.

Even the algorithms. Even the platforms. Even the future itself, it all bends to the questions we dare to ask.

Every system was made by people.

And it can be remade.
By all of us.

This is our moment.

Epilogue – Our Moment

If you've made it here, this story found you.

Three years ago, I began this journey, writing, erasing, rewriting. Whole chapters shifted like sand. The facts were there, but facts rarely move us.

Stories do. And we are a species of storytellers. Maybe the world was waiting for a new one, a hero we could believe in, a journey we hadn't dared to imagine . . . or even look for.

That's when Esra appeared. In many ways, his journey is yours. Maybe you've felt it too, the sense that the world isn't what it seems. That something deeper waits beneath the surface. That the future we've been told is already written . . . might not be the one we truly want.

When Esra began to question, to remember, to reconnect, it wasn't fiction. It was a mirror. A reminder that we've all forgotten something.

His path was imagined, but the facts, and what we can do next, are not. The technologies are real; they already exist. What's missing isn't innovation, but intention, and the will to act differently.

You've glimpsed both worlds:

One grey and restless, data slipping away like smoke, identities scattered, learning locked in dusty rooms. The other alive with colour, data held close, intelligence shared, learning alive in every street and voice.

Not as commodities, but as sacred reflections of who we are, who we've been, and who we could still become.

Financial tools built on your data, for your benefit.
Your AI, not extracting from you, but expanding you.
Healthcare that prevents, because it knows who you are.
Education that unlocks potential, not just passing exams, helping us thrive in life.

A future shaped by our data, ideas, and intelligence, built for everyone.
A world where wisdom is shared, potential unlocked, and the impossible becomes real.

This isn't a fight against Big Tech. Get this right, and we all win. Technology becomes what it was meant to be, an enabler, not the driver.

The future is not inevitable; it's the sum of what we choose to build, protect, share, and leave behind.

Why Our Moment?
Because history won't give us this chance twice.
Technology has arrived with the power to transform our world. For the first time, we stand at a crossroads, to use this moment as a catalyst to evolve outdated systems and mindsets that no longer serve today's world or the one we need to build for tomorrow.

This isn't just for today, it's for generations. **Our Moment** isn't about a single story.
It's about a shift, a generation that says: *We remember who we are. We will not be automated out of our own humanity.*
There's still so much we can do, when we think differently, lead boldly, and let technology be our partner, not our replacement.
My hope is that you carry this not just in your mind, but in your choices.
In your data.
In your conversations.
In how you teach, how you lead, how you live.

This is our moment.
Let's make it count.

But like every good story, this is not the end.
It's just the beginning!

Michael Clark

The Voice That Remains

*"Progress lies not in enhancing what is,
but in advancing toward what will be."*

— Gibran

The world held its breath.

In silence, not stillness.

Fingers hovered above keyboards. Cups paused halfway to lips.
Streets slowed. Crowds gathered under neon digital billboards.
Markets froze mid-ticker.

From mountaintop villages to orbiting stations, they watched.
Every screen. Every time zone. Every language.

This wasn't a moment.
It was *the* moment.

And at the center of it all, the chamber.

A vast, circular coliseum buried beneath the capital.
A fusion of history and hypertech.

Walls carved from centuries-old stone.
Ceilings of translucent glass curved upward into a dome, where
constellations pulsed with shifting data trails.
Columns embedded with fibre optics shimmered with coded light.

And just beyond the glass, drones hovered silently.
Cycling lenses blinked red and blue as they filmed every angle.
Some floated still, others patrolled like watchful spirits.

Rain traced slow lines down the dome above them.
A thin fog coiled at the floor's edge. Not smoke, humidity, alive
and humming from the temperature-calibrated air.

The room full. Thousands. Maybe more.

Tiered seating stretched into darkness. Delegates. Military brass. Visionaries. Dissenters. Generational leaders sat shoulder to shoulder in polished stone rows.

Some wore robes. Others tailored suits, neural-linked lenses, ceremonial armour.
Some came curious. Others came ready to resist.

But all came.

A heavy hush hung in the air, like a storm about to speak.

Then came the doors.

They parted slowly, hydraulics barely audible over the breath of the room. And there he was.

Esra.

His silhouette paused at the threshold. The light from behind cast him in near-silhouette. He stepped forward. Slowly. Deliberately.
A year had passed since the Stranger disappeared.
Since the book closed, and the observatory dimmed.

He was no longer the boy who chased answers.
In his place was someone quieter. Clearer.
A young man carrying the weight of hope in his hands.

His dark blue suit, minimal. The collar slightly undone.
Shoes newly worn. Polished, but not polished by others.

On his wrist: the memory key, blinking softly with a pulse of pale white light.

No music played.
Just footsteps.

Flashbulbs strobed from hidden corners, like stars trying to capture a comet.
Outside the glass, drone-lights shifted, struggling to follow his movement.
He passed through rows of monumental faces.
Near the front: Theo. A simple nod, the kind men give when words aren't enough.

Further down, his mother.
She didn't rise. She didn't cry. She didn't need to.
Her eyes held everything.

Then, he saw them.

Scattered like constellations across the chamber: Dr. Morgan.
Dr. Kai. Sienna. The Steward. The librarian. The repairman. The
bookstore owner.

Each still. Watching. Witnesses.
No applause. No smiles.

Just quiet, reverent presence.

He reached the platform.

A great circular bench, black stone and steel, waited before him.

Behind it sat men and women from every corner of power.
Architects of systems they no longer understood.
Eyes sharp. Expressions unreadable.
And at their center, the man in charge.
Tall. Silver-eyed.
Robed in tradition and embedded tech.
He studied Esra with a gaze honed by decades of power.
He raised the gavel.

CRACK.

"Order."

The echoes didn't bounce, they hung.

Esra took one breath. Deep. Clean. The kind that only comes
before you change everything.

He stepped up to the mic.

The drones adjusted mid-air. Their lenses whirred in unison.

The room dimmed.
And from above, the dome flickered, showing the Earth.

Blue. Alive. Fragile. Glowing.

The world leaned in.

Then . . .

A movement.

Far back, in the topmost tier, a shadow passed.

Unannounced. Unregistered.

A hooded figure walked slowly down the steps. Unhurried.
Unbothered.

The Stranger.

He moved like time forgot him.
He found a seat, dead center at the back. Crossed one leg over
the other.

Esra looked up.

Their eyes met for a moment that felt like memory and prophecy
at once.

The Stranger tipped his hat and nodded once.

Esra smiled. Soft. Certain.
He turned back to the bench.
The old world stared back, familiar, unchallenged, unchanged.
A system that never questioned itself.
Until someone came with nothing to prove.
Only something to offer.
The chamber held still. Not in awe, but anticipation.

The man leaned forward. His voice lower now. No challenge. Just
the question behind everything.

"Then tell me, Esra . . .
Why are you here?"

Esra looked out at them. The watchers. The doubters.
The forgotten. The world.

He turned back to the mic.
"I'm here," he said, voice even, clear.
"To see if the world remembers how to dream."

The bulbs flashed.
A hum flickered through the room.
No one moved.
Not even the drones outside.

And for a moment the world really did stop.

About Michael Clark

Michael Clark is an author and industry pioneer who believes the greatest untapped resource in the world isn't oil, money, or technology, it's human potential. His career began in the boardrooms of Fortune 500 companies and led to advising governments and smart cities, where he discovered a bigger truth: progress is not measured by faster machines, but by how deeply we unlock what people can become.

Along the way, he saw how data, AI, and education could be reimagined to open doors we've long overlooked. Today, he helps industries, nations, and individuals prepare for the next economy where data becomes an asset, AI serves humanity, and education awakens hidden abilities. His mission is simple: to help the world rediscover its potential.

www.ingramcontent.com/pod-product-compliance
Lightning Source LLC
Chambersburg PA
CBHW030641020726
47493CB00006B/1822